THE
MIDNIGHT GANG

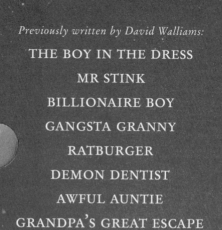

David Walliams

THE
MIDNIGHT
GANG

Illustrated by Tony Ross

HarperCollins *Children's Books*

First published in Great Britain by
HarperCollins Children's Books in 2016
HarperCollins Children's Books is a division of
HarperCollins Publishers Ltd,
HarperCollins Publishers
1 London
Bridge
Street
London
SE1 9GF

The HarperCollins website address is:
www.harpercollins.co.uk

5

Cover lettering

of author's name

copyright ©

Quentin Blake 2010

Illustrations copyright © Tony Ross 2016

Text copyright © David Walliams 2016

HB ISBN 978–0–00–816461–4
TPB ISBN 978–0–00–818857–3

David Walliams and Tony
Ross assert the moral right
to be identified as the author
and illustrator of this work.

Printed and bound in England by Clays Ltd, St Ives plc

MIX
Paper from
responsible sources
FSC www.fsc.org **FSC® C007454**

FSC™ is a non-profit international organisation established to promote
the responsible management of the world's forests. Products carrying the
FSC label are independently certified to assure consumers that they come
from forests that are managed to meet the social, economic and
ecological needs of present and future generations,
and other controlled sources.

Find out more about HarperCollins and the environment at
www.harpercollins.co.uk/green

For Wendy and Henry, two keen readers
and future writers.
David x

⇒ THANK YOUS →

I would like to thank:

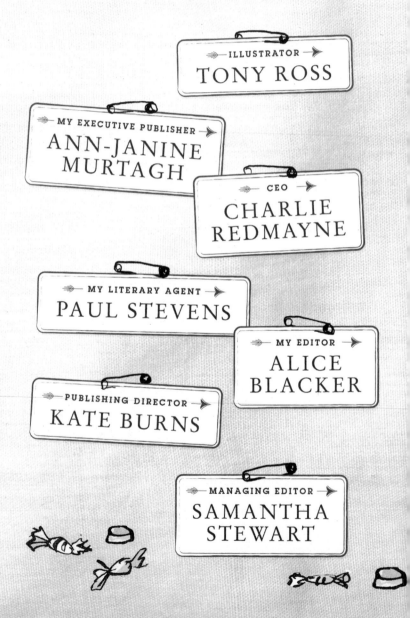

⇒ ILLUSTRATOR →
TONY ROSS

⇒ MY EXECUTIVE PUBLISHER →
ANN-JANINE MURTAGH

⇒ CEO →
CHARLIE REDMAYNE

⇒ MY LITERARY AGENT →
PAUL STEVENS

⇒ MY EDITOR →
ALICE BLACKER

⇒ PUBLISHING DIRECTOR →
KATE BURNS

⇒ MANAGING EDITOR →
SAMANTHA STEWART

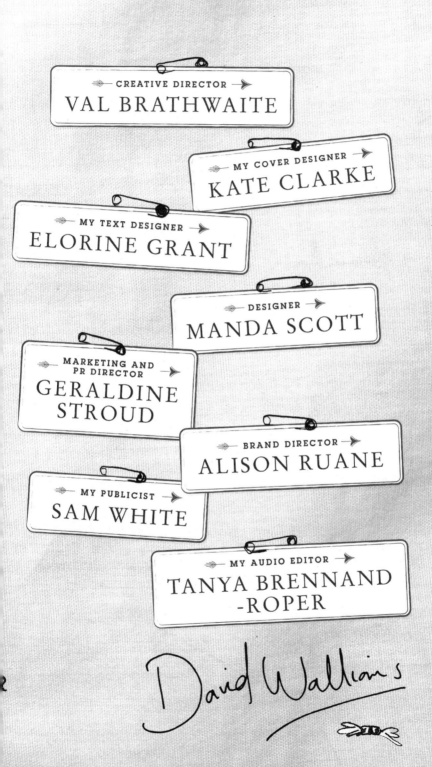

CREATIVE DIRECTOR →
VAL BRATHWAITE

MY COVER DESIGNER →
KATE CLARKE

MY TEXT DESIGNER →
ELORINE GRANT

DESIGNER →
MANDA SCOTT

MARKETING AND
PR DIRECTOR →
GERALDINE
STROUD

BRAND DIRECTOR →
ALISON RUANE

MY PUBLICIST →
SAM WHITE

MY AUDIO EDITOR →
TANYA BRENNAND
-ROPER

David Walliams

Welcome to the world of the Midnight Gang.

This is **LORD FUNT HOSPITAL**, in London, England. It was built many years ago and should have been demolished many years ago. The hospital was named in honour of its founder, the late Lord Funt.

THIS WAY UP

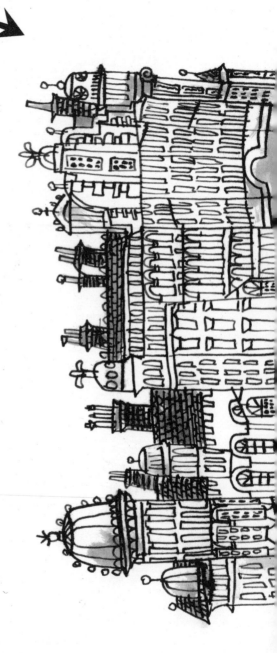

LORD FUNT
HOSPITAL

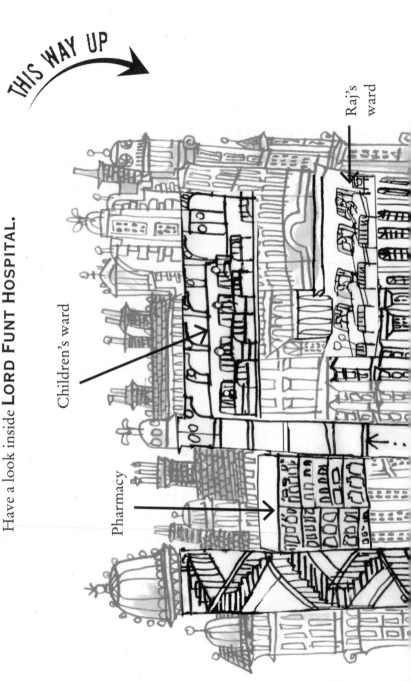

THIS WAY UP

Have a look inside **LORD FUNT HOSPITAL.**

Raj's ward

Children's ward

Pharmacy

Sir Quentin Strillers's office

...enry's ward

Basement

Gift shop

Meet the patients in the children's ward, high up on the forty-fourth floor of the hospital.

This is Tom. He is twelve and goes to a posh boarding school. He has hurt his head.

Amber is twelve. She has broken both of her arms and both of her legs, so has been in a wheelchair for some time.

Robin is also twelve. He is recovering from an operation to save his eyesight, and for now can't see a thing.

George is eleven and from the East End of London, which makes him a cockney. He is recovering from having his tonsils taken out in an operation.

Sally is just ten and the youngest of the group. Because she is so ill, Sally spends most of her time sleeping.

Downstairs in one of the grown-ups' wards is the oldest patient in the hospital – ninety-nine-year-old Nelly.

Hundreds of people work at LORD FUNT HOSPITAL. Among them are:

Porter. A lonely figure, whose real name is a mystery. His job is to move people and things around the hospital, which he never seems to leave.

Matron. Despite running the children's ward, she doesn't like children at all.

Doctor Luppers has just become a doctor, and is rather easy to fool.

Tootsie is the hospital's dinner lady. She brings meals round on a trolley to all the patients.

Nurse Meese is the tired-looking nurse, who never ever seems to get a night off work.

Dilly is one of the hospital's cleaners. You can always tell where she has cleaned as there will be a long trail of fag ash.

Mr Cod is the old chemist. He has a hearing aid and thick glasses. Mr Cod runs the pharmacy in the hospital.

Sir Quentin Strillers is the upper-class
hospital principal, and is in charge of everyone
and everything.

From outside the hospital there is Mr Thews, the headmaster of Tom's school, **_St Willet's Boarding School for Boys_**.

Midnight
is the time
when all the
children are fast asleep,

except of course for...

the Midnight Gang!

That is the time when their

adventures

are just

beginning.

CHAPTER 1

MONSTER MAN

"Aaarrrggghhh!" screamed the boy.

The most monstrous face he had ever seen was peering down at him. It was the face of a man, but it was completely lopsided. One side was larger than it should have been, and the other was smaller. The face smiled as if to calm the boy down, only to reveal a set of broken and rotten teeth. This made the boy even more scared than before.

"Aaaaarrrrrggggghhhhh!!!!!" he screamed again.

"You will be all right, young sir. Please try and be calm," slurred the man.

His face was so misshapen, that so was his speech.

Who was this man and where was he taking the boy?

It was only then the boy realised he was lying on his back, staring straight up. It felt almost as if he was floating. But something was **rattling**. *He* was **rattling.** The boy realised he must be lying on a trolley. A trolley with wonky wheels.

His head clouded with questions.

Where was he?

How did he get here?

Why couldn't he remember a thing?

And, most importantly, who was this terrifying man-monster?

The trolley travelled slowly down the long corridor. The boy could hear the sound of something being dragged along the floor. It sounded like the *squeak* of a shoe.

He looked down. The man was limping. Just like his face, one side of his body was smaller than the other,

so the man was dragging his withered leg along with him. It looked like every movement might be painful.

BANG!

A pair of tall doors swung open and the trolley trundled into a room and came to a stop. Then some curtains were drawn round the boy.

"I hope that wasn't too uncomfortable, young sir," said the man. The boy thought it was curious that this man called him "sir". He had never been called "sir" in his life. He was only twelve. "Sir" was a title reserved only for teachers at his boarding school. "Now you wait here. I'm just the porter. Let me get the nurse. Nurse!"

As he lay there, the boy felt strangely disconnected from his own body. It felt limp. Lifeless.

The pain, though, was in his head. It was throbbing. Hot. If the feeling could be a colour, it would be red.

A bright, hot, raging red.

The pain was so intense he closed his eyes.

When he opened them, he realised he was staring straight up at a bright fluorescent light. This made his head ache even more than before.

Then he heard the sound of footsteps approaching.

The curtain was whisked back.

A large older lady in a blue-and-white uniform with a hat leaned over and examined the boy's head. Dark circles framed her bloodshot eyes. Grey wiry hair squatted on her head. Her face was red raw, as if she had scrubbed it with a cheese grater. In brief, she had the appearance of someone who had not slept for a week, and was angry about it.

"Oh deary me! Oh deary, deary me. Oh deary, deary, deary me…" she muttered to nobody in particular.

In his confused state the boy took a moment to realise this woman was in fact dressed as a nurse.

At last the boy realised where he was. A hospital. He had never been in one before, except the day he was born. And he couldn't remember that.

The boy's eyes drifted up to the lady's name badge: NURSE MEESE, **LORD FUNT HOSPITAL**.

"That is a bump. A big bump. A very big bump. Now, does this hurt?" she said as she poked the boy hard on his head with her finger.

"**O**ooo**www**!" he screamed, so loudly it echoed along the corridor.

"Some slight pain," muttered the nurse. "Now, just let me get the doctor. Doctor!"

The curtain was whisked across, and then back again.

As the boy lay there staring at the ceiling, he could hear the sound of footsteps departing.

"Doctor!" she barked out again, now some way down the corridor.

"Coming, Nurse!" came a voice from far off.

"Quickly!" she shouted.

"Sorry!" said the voice.

Then there was the sound of footsteps approaching at speed.

The curtain was whisked back.

A young pointy-faced man breezed in, his long white coat trailing behind him.

"Oh dear. Oh dear, oh dear," announced a posh voice. It was a doctor, and he was somewhat out of breath at having had to run. Looking up, the boy read the man's name badge – DOCTOR LUPPERS.

"That is a big bump. Does this hurt?" The man took

out a pencil from his breast pocket. He then held one end and tapped the boy's head with it.

"Oooowwww!" the boy screamed again. It wasn't as bad as being jabbed by a gnarly old finger, but it still hurt.

"Sorry, sorry, sorry! Please don't report me. I've only just graduated as a doctor, you see."

"I won't," muttered the boy.

"Are you sure?"

"Quite sure!"

"Thank you. Now I need to make sure I cross the 'i's and dot the 't's. I just have this little admissions form to fill in." The man then proceeded to roll out a form that looked as if it might take a week to complete.

The boy sighed.

"So, young man," began the
doctor in a singsong tone
that he hoped might make
this boring task fun,
"what is your name?"

The boy's mind went
blank.

He had never forgotten
his own name before.

"Name?" asked the doctor again.

But, try as he might, the boy couldn't remember it.

"I don't know," he spluttered.

CHAPTER 2

HERE OR THERE

A look of panic swept across the doctor's face. "Oh dear," he said. "There are a hundred and ninety-two questions on this form and we are still stuck on question one."

"I'm sorry," replied the boy. As he lay on the hospital trolley, a tear rolled down his cheek. He felt like such a failure, not even being able to remember his own name.

"Oh no! You're crying!" said the doctor. "Please don't cry! The hospital principal could come by and think that I have upset you!"

The boy did his best to stop. Doctor Luppers searched his pockets for a tissue. Unable to locate one, he dabbed the boy's eyes with the form.

"Oh no! Now the form's wet!" he exclaimed. He then began blowing on the form to try and dry it. This made the boy laugh. "Oh good!" said the man. "You are smiling! Now, look, I am sure we can find out your name. Does it begin with an **A?**"

The boy was pretty sure it didn't. "I don't think so."

"B?"

The boy shook his head.

"C?"

He shook his head again.

"This could take some time," muttered the doctor under his breath.

"T!" exclaimed the boy.

"You would like a cup of tea?"

"No! My name. It begins with a **T!"**

Doctor Luppers smiled as he wrote the first letter on the top of the form. "Let's see if I can guess. **Tim? Ted? Terry? Tony? Theo? Taj?** No, you don't look like a **Taj**... I've got it! **Tina?!"**

All these suggestions firing at the boy clouded his mind, making it more difficult for him to remember, but finally his own name came shining through.

"**Tom!**" said Tom.

"**Tom!**" exclaimed the doctor, as if he was about to have guessed it. He wrote down the next two letters. "So what do they call you? **Thomas? Tommy? Big Tom? Little Tom? Tom Thumb?**"

"**Tom**," replied Tom wearily. Tom had already said his name was Tom.

"Do you have a surname?"

"It begins with a **C**," said the boy.

"Well, at least we have the first letter. It's like doing the crossword!"

"Charper!"

"*Tom Charper!*" said the man, scribbling it down on the form. "That's question one done. Just a hundred and ninety-one to go. Now, who brought you to the hospital today? Are your mummy and daddy here?"

"No," said Tom. He could be sure of that. His parents weren't here. They were never *here*; they were always *there*. For some years now, they had packed their only child off to a posh boarding school deep in the English countryside: **St Willet's Boarding School for Boys**.

Tom's father earned a lot of money working in desert countries far away, extracting oil from the ground, and his mother was very good at spending that money. Tom would only see them on school holidays, usually in a different country each time. Even though Tom had travelled alone for hours to see them, his father would often still have to work all day

and his mother would leave him with a nanny while she went shopping for more shoes and handbags. The boy would be lavished with presents upon arrival – a new train set, a model plane or a knight's suit of armour. But with nobody to play with Tom would get bored quickly. All he really wanted was to spend time with Mum and Dad, but time was the one thing they never ever gave him.

"No. Mother and Father are abroad," answered Tom. "I am not sure who brought me to the hospital today. It must have been a teacher."

"Oooh!" said Doctor Luppers excitedly. "Might it have been your games teacher? There was a man in the waiting area dressed as a cricket umpire with a straw hat and long white jacket, which I thought was unusual, as we tend not to have cricket matches in the waiting area."

"That must have been my games teacher, Mr Carsey, yes."

Doctor Luppers's eyes flicked down to his form. They flashed with panic once again. "Oh dear, it only says 'parent', 'guardian', 'friend' or 'other' on the form. What am I going to do?"

"Tick 'other'," instructed the boy, taking charge.

"Thank you!" said the doctor, looking relieved. "Thank you so, so much. What is the nature of your injury?"

"A bump on the head."

"Of course, yes!" replied Doctor Luppers as he scribbled that down on the form. "Now, next question, would you say the general appearance of **LORD FUNT HOSPITAL** has 'been lower than your expectations', 'has met your expectations', 'has exceeded your expectations' or 'has greatly exceeded your expectations'?"

"What was the first one again?" asked Tom. The pain in his head made it hard for him to think straight.

"Ooh, that's 'been lower than your expectations'."

"What is?"

"The general appearance of the hospital."

"I've only seen the ceiling so far," sighed the boy.

"And how would you rate the general appearance of the ceiling?"

"Fine."

"I'll put that it 'has met your expectations'. Next question, would you say that the care you have received today at the hospital has been, 'poor', 'fine', 'good', 'very good' or in fact 'too good'?"

"It's been all right," replied Tom.

"Mmm, sorry, but 'all right' isn't on the form."

"'Good' then?"

"Not 'very good'?" said Doctor Luppers, a hint of pleading in his voice. "It would be nice to say I got a 'very good' on my first week."

Tom sighed. "Put 'too good' then."

"Oooh, thank you!" replied the doctor, his eyes dancing with delight. "No one ever gets a 'too good'!

Though I worry whether 'too good' might actually be a bad thing. Can I just put 'very'?"

"Yes, put whatever you like."

"I'll put 'very good'. Thank you very much! This will go down very well with the hospital principal, Sir Quentin Strillers. Now, next question. We're racing through them now. Would you recommend **LORD FUNT HOSPITAL** to family and friends, 'with a heavy heart', 'half-heartedly', 'wholeheartedly' or 'very wholeheartedly'?"

Suddenly Nurse Meese bustled through the curtains. "There isn't time for all your stupid questions, Doctor!"

The man put his hand up to his face as though he thought he was going to be slapped. "Don't hurt me!"

"You silly boy! As if I would!" replied the nurse, before clouting him round the ear hard with her thick, heavy hand.

"OW!" screamed Doctor Luppers. "That hurt!"

"Well, at least you are in the right place for an

injury! Ha ha!" The woman laughed to herself, and almost managed a smile. "I need this station back right now! I have a newsagent being rushed here in an ambulance who managed to staple his own fingers together. Stupid man!"

"Oh no!" replied the doctor. "I can't stand the sight of blood."

"Get this boy out of here before I'm back or I will clout you round the other ear!" With that, Nurse Meese whipped back the curtain and stomped off down the corridor.

"OK," began Doctor Luppers, "let me speed this up as much as I can." The man began speaking very fast. "Bad swelling. Keep you here for a few nights. Just to be safe. Hope you don't mind."

Tom didn't mind staying at the hospital at all. Anything to miss time at his dreaded boarding school. It was one of the most expensive schools in the country, and so most of the boys who went there were exceedingly posh. Tom's parents were rich because of his father's well-paid job abroad, but the family were not posh at all. Lots of the boys looked down their aristocratic noses at Tom.

"I am just going to send you up to the children's ward right away. Nice and peaceful up there. You should get a good night's sleep. Porter?"

Tom froze in fear as the terrifying man limped back in.

"Yes, Doctor Luppers, sir?" he slurred.

"Take… sorry, sorry, sorry… What was your name again?"

"Tom!" replied Tom.

"Take Tom up to the children's ward."

CHAPTER 3

BUMP

The porter wheeled the trolley Tom was lying on into the hospital lift. The old misshapen man hummed quietly to himself as he pressed a button for the top floor. Tom hated being alone with him. It wasn't as if he had done anything **SCARY**; he just *looked* **SCARY**.

The boy had never seen anyone so spectacularly ugly before. Yes, there were teachers at his posh boarding school that were so unfortunate-looking they had been given cruel nicknames by the boys, but none was as scary-looking as the porter.

There was:

Mrs Rabbit

The Dome
of Doom

Mr Dead-
Squirrel-On-
His-Head

The Hairy
Gnome

Mrs Goggle-Eyes

Dr Octopus

Mr Clown-Shoes

The Dinosaur

Miss Hooter

Professor
Comb-Over

$PING!$ The lift doors closed.

The porter smiled at Tom, but the boy looked the other way. He couldn't bear to look at the man. He seemed even creepier when he smiled. Those rotten and misshapen teeth looked like they could crunch through your bones. Tom's eyes scanned the man's

name badge. Unlike the nurse
and doctor he had already met,
this badge didn't have a name
on it, but just the man's job.

As the lift trundled slowly upwards, Tom's world
gradually began to take shape. Little by little, he
began piecing together the events that had brought
him here.

It had been a blazing hot summer's day and he had
been playing cricket on the school pitch. The boy
lifted his head slightly and looked down. He was still
wearing his cricket whites.

Despite his school priding itself on always coming
top in cricket and rugby in the country, Tom wasn't
good at sports. The school celebrated all its sporting
heroes with cups and trophies and medals and special
mentions by the headmaster in assembly. A boy who
much preferred to hide himself away in the corner of
the school library with some dusty old books like Tom
could easily feel like a nobody.

Tom was miserable at school, and would wish the time away. *If only the days and nights would pass quicker*, he would often think to himself. The boy was only twelve, but he longed to leave childhood behind forever. Then he would be a grown-up and would not have to go to school any more.

The school played cricket in the summer, and Tom immediately discovered the best part of the game for the reluctant sportsman… fielding. The boy would always place himself at the very far edge of the pitch. So far out that Tom could indulge in his favourite pastime – daydreaming. So far out he could daydream the afternoon away. So far out there was little or no chance of the heavy red leather ball ever coming your way.

Well, that was Tom's thinking.

This time he was wrong.

Very wrong.

As the numbers of the floors flashed past in the lift, the last thing Tom remembered flashed past in his mind.

A heavy red leather ball

flying through the air straight towards

him at terrific speed.

THUD

Then everything went dark.

PinG!

"This is your stop, young sir! Top floor! Home

of **LORD FUNT HOSPITAL**'s children's ward!"

slurred the porter.

As the lift doors opened, the trolley was rolled

out. The porter pushed Tom down yet another long

corridor before a pair of tall doors banged open.

The pair was inside the children's ward.

"Welcome to your new home," said the porter.

CHAPTER 4
THE CHILDREN'S WARD

Tom raised his swollen head a little to take his first look at what was his new home, the children's ward of **LORD FUNT HOSPITAL**. There were four other children in the ward. They were all sitting or lying on their beds. All were silent, and no one paid this new boy much attention. Boredom hung in the still, stuffy air. It was more like an old people's home than a children's ward.

In the nearest bed was a plump-looking boy in an old pair of spotty pyjamas that were too small for him. He was flicking through a dog-eared picture book of helicopters, and sneakily munching on some chocolates he had hidden under his bed sheet. The name **George** was chalked on a blackboard above his bed.

Next to him was a short, slight boy with neatly
combed ginger hair. He must have had an operation
on his eyes as they were covered with bandages. So
covered, in fact, that it would be impossible to see

anything. A tall pile of classical music CDs and a CD player sat on his side table. The boy's pyjamas were much smarter than George's, and he wore them neatly with the top button done up. Over his bed in chalk was the name **Robin**.

Across the ward from him was a girl with a bob of black hair and round glasses. Startlingly, she had both her legs and arms in plaster. All four of her limbs were being held aloft by a complex series of pulleys and winches. She looked like a puppet on strings. On her blackboard it read **Amber**.

Then in the far corner of the ward, away from the other children, Tom noticed a sorrowful figure. It was a girl, but it was hard to tell her age as it looked as if illness had weakened her. A few wispy strands of hair sat on top of her head. Above her bed was chalked the name **Sally**.

"Say hello to everyone, young sir," prompted the porter.

Tom felt shy, so muttered, "Hello," as quietly as he could get away with, without being told to repeat himself.

There was a vague murmur of "hellos" in return, though Sally remained silent.

"This must be your bed, right here," slurred the porter as he wheeled the trolley over. Expertly the boy was rolled from the trolley to the bed.

"Are you comfortable?" asked the porter, plumping up a pillow.

Tom didn't answer. It wasn't comfortable at all. It was like lying on a concrete slab with a brick for a pillow. Even the trolley was more comfortable. It was stupid for Tom to pretend not to hear the porter, as he was standing right next to him. The man was so close that Tom could smell him. In fact, the boy was sure the whole ward could smell him. The man was rather pongy, like he hadn't washed for quite some time. His clothes were tired and worn. His shoes were falling apart and his work overall was thick with grease and grime. He looked like he might be homeless.

"So this is the world's worst cricketer?" came a voice. The children in the ward tensed and **shivered** at the sound.

Then a tall, thin lady stepped out of her office at the

far end of the room. It was Matron, the senior nurse who was in charge of the ward. Slowly and surely she made her way down the row of beds towards Tom, her high heels clunking on the floor.

From a distance, Matron looked like she was beautiful. Her long blonde hair had been sprayed perfectly in place, her face was shiny with make-up and her teeth were sparkling white. However, when she got nearer to Tom, the boy realised that her smile was fake. Her eyes were two large black pools, a window into the darkness within. Matron's perfume was so sickly sweet it burned the children's throats as she passed by.

"You are meant to catch a cricket ball! Not header it!" said the lady. "Stupid, stupid child! **Ha ha ha!**" No one laughed except her. It certainly didn't sound funny to Tom, whose head was still throbbing with pain.

"That cricket ball left a very nasty bump, Madam Matron," slurred the porter. His voice was cracking a little, as if he was nervous of the woman. "I think young sir should have an X-ray first thing in the morning."

"I don't need your opinion, thank you!" snapped Matron. In an instant, her face didn't seem that beautiful after all, as it twisted into a snarl. "You are nothing more than a lowly porter, lowest of the low. You don't know the first thing about caring for the patients. So in future keep your mouth shut!"

The porter lowered his head, and the other children exchanged nervous looks. It was clear this lady intimidated them all too.

With a flick of her hand, Matron brushed the porter aside, and he stumbled a little to steady himself.

"Let me look at this bump," she said as she peered over the boy. "Mmm, yes, that is a nasty bump. You should have an X-ray first thing in the morning."

The porter rolled his eyes at Tom, but once again the boy didn't react.

Without even so much as glancing at him, Matron said to the man, "Porter, you may go before you stink out my ward!"

The porter sighed before giving a brief smile and nod to all the children on the ward.

"Quickly!" shouted the woman, and the man limped off as fast as he could, dragging his withered leg behind him.

Tom began longing to be back at school. The children's ward seemed an utterly **miserable** place to be.

CHAPTER 5
PINK-FRILLY-NIGHTDRESS BOY

Matron launched into what seemed like a very well-rehearsed speech. A speech she must have given to all her new patients.

"Now, young man, this is MY ward and these are MY rules. Lights out at 8pm sharp. No talking after lights out. No reading under the covers. No eating of sweeties. If I do hear the rustle of sweet papers in the dark, I will confiscate them on the spot. Yes, that includes you, George!"

The podgy boy immediately stopped chewing, and kept his mouth tightly shut so Matron couldn't see he was chewing a chocolate at that very moment.

The woman continued at quite a pace. Her words snapped like the crack of a whip.

"No getting out of bed. No visits to the toilet during the night; that is what the bedpan is for. You will find a bedpan under your bed. There is a bell on the wall by your head. Ring the bell in the night only in an absolute emergency. Do you understand me?"

"Yes," replied Tom. It was like being told off before you had actually even done anything wrong.

"Now, have you brought any pyjamas with you?" she asked.

"No," replied Tom. "I must have been rushed here in an ambulance when I was knocked out on the cricket pitch. I didn't have a chance to pack anything, so I've just got my cricket kit that I came in. I don't mind sleeping in it."

Matron's lips curled in horror. "Repulsive child! You are as bad as that disgusting excuse for a human being, the porter. He smells like he sleeps in his clothes. Ha ha! Can we call your parents to bring some pyjamas for you?"

Tom shook his head sorrowfully.

"Why not?"

"My mother and father live abroad."

"Where?"

The boy hesitated before answering. "I am not sure."

"You are not sure?!" said Matron loudly so everyone could hear. It was as if she wanted all the children in the ward to enjoy the new boy being humiliated as much as she did.

"They move around a lot for my father's work. I know it's somewhere with a desert."

"Well, that narrows it down!" she snarled sarcastically. "You don't even know what country your own parents live in! Well, you will fit right in here. The children in this ward are all ones whose parents don't ever visit for one reason or another. They are either too poor to travel like Amber's, or too ill like Robin's, or live too far away like Sally's. George has the best reason, though. Would you care to explain why your parents never visit, George?"

"Nah," the boy muttered in his cockney accent. The accent struck Tom, as no one at his boarding school talked like George. The poor boy looked desperately embarrassed. "Don't…"

"George's father is in prison! For robbery, no less! So if anything goes missing in the ward we'll know who to blame! Like father, like son! Ha ha!"

"I ain't a thief!" shouted George.

"No need to be so sensitive, child. It's just my little joke!"

"Well, it ain't funny!" he replied.

"Ooh!" she added mockingly. "I've touched a nerve! Now I have an idea for you, Tom. Let me find you something to wear in my lost-property box."

With a glint in her eye, Matron turned on her heel and disappeared into her office. Moments later, she emerged with her hands behind her back and a suspicious grin on her face.

"I am awfully sad to say, Tom, that I don't have any pyjamas to fit you!" she said. "So you will just have to wear this!"

From behind her back, Matron produced a pink, frilly nightdress. The **smug** grin on her face became even **smugger**.

Tom looked at the pink, frilly nightdress with horror. If the other boys in his boarding school ever heard about him wearing it, he would never ever live it down. In fact, he would be forever known as **Pink-Frilly-Nightdress Boy**.

"Please just let me keep my cricket gear on, Matron," pleaded Tom.

"I said *no*!" snapped Matron.

"I got pyjamas 'e can borrow," said George.

"Don't be ridiculous, child!" replied the lady in a flash. "Look at the size of you, boy! They will be far too big! Your pyjamas would be too big for an elephant! Ha ha ha!"

Once again, no one laughed except Matron.

"Now get this on right away or I will report you to the principal of the hospital, Sir Quentin Strillers. He would take a very dim view of a boy like you and could have you thrown out on the street!" said the lady as she whisked the curtains round the boy's bed. She stayed on the outside, leaving Tom to try to wriggle out of his clothes and into the nightdress on his own.

"Quickly!" ordered Matron.

"I am nearly there!" called out Tom as he pulled the thing over his head. "OK!" he said, even though he felt far from OK.

Matron then whisked the curtains back to reveal Tom.

There stood **Pink-Frilly-Nightdress Boy** in all his pink-frilly-nightdress glory.

"Actually, it suits ya!" said George.

"I so wish I could see it," murmured Robin.

"No you don't!" replied Amber.

CHAPTER 6

UP TO NO GOOD

Tom had had some humiliating things happen to him at his school over the years.

There was the time when...

his shorts split while he was doing gymnastics...

his clay spun off the wheel in Pottery class and hit his art teacher on the face, sending her flying...

he bent over to pick up a book from the floor in the library and he blew off loudly...

he left the toilet cubicle with the toilet roll trailing

from the back of his trousers...

he was in the school cafeteria and he slipped on some

gravy and landed headfirst in a blancmange...

he was holding his violin the wrong way round in music class, wondering why he wasn't making a sound until he realised the strings were facing down...

some of the older boys hid his games kit so he had to play rugby in his pants...

he had to put on a tight-fitting all-in-one bodysuit, with a tail stuck to his bottom. He was meant to be a cat, and had to sing and dance for a production of the musical *Cats*...

he thought it
might be a trick
question when
his Maths teacher
asked him what
2 + 2 was, so he
answered 5...

chalk dust set off a sneezing fit, and he sneezed right
in his headmaster's face, covering Mr Thews in snot.

But now here he was, standing in the middle of a hospital ward, wearing a pink, frilly nightdress.

"It fits you perfectly!" laughed Matron. Once again, it was only her that was laughing. Then she checked her watch, which was pinned to her uniform. "One minute past eight. Way past all your bedtimes! Right, children. Lights out!"

Matron began to march in the direction of her office at the end of the ward.

As if they were all playing Grandma's Footsteps, she suddenly turned round after a few paces to see if any of the children had moved. Then she did it again. And again. Matron gave one last swivel-eyed look at the children, before switching off the light.

CLICK!

The ward descended into darkness. Tom hated the dark. He was relieved that some light came from the giant clock face of the Houses of Parliament, not far away from the hospital across the rooftops of London. People called the clock tower "Big Ben", after the huge bell inside it that chimed every hour.

BONG! The light from the clock face glowed eerily through the tall windows.

There was also a small desk lamp in Matron's office. The lady sat there behind the glass, staring out into the gloom. She was scanning the beds in the children's ward for any sign of movement.

Silence.

Then out of that silence Tom heard a sound. It was the sound of a tin opening. Then followed the sound of paper rustling. But not just any paper. It sounded like the crinkly silver paper that sweets are wrapped in. Then Tom heard the sound of munching.

Tom hadn't eaten since lunchtime, and he had barely eaten his lunch as school dinners were so disgusting. Today it had been liver and boiled beetroot, followed by stewed rhubarb. Lying there on his hospital bed, Tom could feel his tummy rumbling. When he heard another sweet being unwrapped, and another, he couldn't help calling out softly in the dark, "Please can I have one?"

" *Shush!*" came a voice back. Tom was pretty sure it was coming from George's bed.

"Please?" whispered Tom. "I haven't eaten for ages."

" *Shush!*" came another voice. "Any louder and you'll get us all into trouble."

"I only want one!" said Tom.

The boy must have spoken too loudly as at that moment…

CLICK!

…the lights in the children's ward flickered back on.

Blinking at the brightness, Tom could make out Matron rushing out of her office.

"THERE IS NO TALKING AFTER LIGHTS OUT!" she shouted.

"Now *who* was talking?"

All the children remained silent.

"You must tell me now who was talking or you will all be in deep, deep trouble!"

She scanned the ward for signs of anyone cracking under pressure. She looked to George, who looked guilty.

"Was it you, George?" she demanded.

George shook his head.

"Speak up, boy!"

Even from across the room, Tom could tell George's mouth was full.

George tried to speak, but because of the large quantity of chocolate in his mouth, he couldn't form words. "Mmm, mmm, mmm," he murmured.

"What have you got in your mouth?"

George shook his head and tried to say "nothing" but it came out as, "Mmm, mmm, mmm."

Matron approached his bed like a crocodile stalking its prey. "George! You are meant to be on a strict diet after your operation. But you are scoffing chocolates again, aren't you?"

George shook his head.

The lady whipped back his bed sheet to reveal a large tin of chocolates. The tin was huge. It was the kind that your family might receive at Christmas and would last until next Christmas.

"You greedy pig!" said Matron. "These are confiscated!"

With that, she snatched the tin from his hands and whipped a tissue from a nearby box. "Now spit out the one you have in your mouth."

Reluctantly, the boy did so.

"Who sent you these?" she demanded. "I know it couldn't have been your father. I am not sure they are allowed chocolates in prison!"

Tom could tell George was angry, but the boy was doing his best to keep it in.

"They came from me local newsagent," replied George. "I'm 'is favourite customer."

"I bet you are! Look at the size of you!"

"You see, 'e knows I love these chocolates the most."

"What is this stupid man's name?"

"Raj," replied George.

"Raj what?"

"Raj the newsagent."

"I mean what's his surname, you foolish child?"

"Dunno."

"Well, I will try to trace him and with any luck have

his shop closed down. After your operation, you are forbidden from eating chocolates, George."

"Sorry, Matron."

"'Sorry' isn't good enough! The hospital principal, Sir Quentin Strillers, will have to be told about you defying doctor's orders like this, George!"

"Yes, Matron," answered the boy sorrowfully.

"I will deal with you in the morning! Now go to sleep! All of you!"

Matron stalked back towards her office. Once again, like Grandma's Footsteps, she turned round several times to check the children were as still as statues.

CLICK!

The lights went off again, and Matron sat in her office. After a moment, the lady did the most incredible thing. She opened the tin and started scoffing the chocolates herself!

Matron seemed to like the big purple wrapped ones the best, as she made her way through them at quite a pace. She had barely popped one in her mouth when the next one was already being unwrapped ready for scoffing. Time passed and the more she ate, the sleepier she became. By nine o'clock, her eyelids were flickering. Still she ate and ate and ate. Perhaps she hoped the sugar in the chocolates would keep her awake. Strangely, they seemed to be having the opposite effect. By 10pm, her eyes were closing for a few seconds at a time. Still she ate and ate and ate. By 11pm, she was desperately trying to prop up her head in her hands, but it was becoming heavier and heavier and heavier. The scoffing slowed down too, and soon the chocolate mush dribbled out of her mouth and her head hit her desk with a loud...

THUD!

Through the glass, Matron could be heard snoring.

"ZZZZZ, ZZZZZ, ZZZZZ, ZZZZZ..."

The children on the ward all remained silent for a moment. Then out of the darkness someone whispered, "Well done, George."

"I think the plan's workin'!" he whispered back. George's cockney accent made his voice stand out.

"What plan?" asked Tom.

" *Shush!*" came another voice.

"Go to sleep, new boy! Stop poking your nose into other people's business," said a girl. "Now, let's all get ready to go at midnight."

But of course Tom couldn't sleep, especially now he knew the children were up to no good. What was going to happen at midnight?

CHAPTER 7

THE MIDNIGHT HOUR

The glow from the clock face of Big Ben shone through the tall window behind Tom's bed. Suddenly Tom could see shadows flashing through the children's ward. Figures were moving in the darkness.

Tom was frightened and couldn't help but gasp.

"Aaah!"

Just then he felt a hand on his mouth, silencing him.

This made Tom even more frightened.

" Shush!" hissed someone. "Don't make a sound. We don't want anyone wakin' up Matron."

The hand was soft and fleshy and smelled of chocolate, and as Tom's eyes adjusted to the dark he realised it was indeed George's.

Tom's eyes darted over to the matron's office. The

lady was still fast asleep in her chair, her head resting on her desk, snoring away.

"ZZZzz, ZZZzz, ZZZzz, ZZZZzz..."

"Not one sound!" repeated George.

Tom nodded his agreement to the boy, who slowly removed his hand.

Then Tom looked behind him towards the giant clock. He could see across the rooftops of London. It was approaching midnight.

Soon it was clear that it wasn't just George who was out of his bed. Robin was also there, pushing Amber along in a wheelchair. The wheelchair was old and rusty, and even had a flat tyre. Because Robin had bandages over his eyes, he couldn't see a thing. Amber's bandaged legs banged straight into the wall.

"OW!" she cried.

"*Shush!*" said Robin and George. Tom found himself joining in too.

"*Shush!*"

"Let me!" said George. He guided Robin to one side, and then took over the pushing of Amber. Robin put his hand on George's shoulder, and like a rather pitiful conga the trio shuffled out of the ward.

"Where are you going?" asked Tom.

"*Shush!*" the three children replied.

"Can you please stop telling me to '*shush*' all the time!" protested Tom.

"Just go to sleep, new boy!" hissed Amber.

"But..." Tom protested.

"You are not in our gang!" added George.

"But I really want to be in your gang," pleaded Tom.

"Well, you can't be, mate!" replied George.

"But it's not fair!" moaned Tom.

"Please can you turn the volume down, dear!" snapped Robin.

"YES, BE QUIET!" said Amber.

"I am being quiet!" replied Tom.

"You are not being quiet! You are talking and that's not being quiet! We all have to be quiet!" said Amber.

"Then you be quiet!" said Tom.

"Oh for goodness' sake, will you all please be quiet?!" said Robin, a little too loudly.

All the children's heads turned towards the matron's office at the end of the ward. Matron stirred a little at the noise, but didn't wake up. There was a collective sigh of relief.

"The ol' moo shouldn't wake up for a couple of hours at least," said George. "There was one of my special snoozy pellets that Dr Luppers gave me pushed inside each of those chocolates."

"Well done for remembering she liked the purple ones the best," said Amber.

"No point ruinin' a whole tin of chocolates, was there?" replied George with a smirk.

"You crafty devils!" said Tom.

"Why, thank you!" replied Robin, bowing his head as if for applause.

SPECIAL
◆ SNOOZY ◆
PELLETS

"Now, new boy," said Amber, "go back to bed right now. And, remember, you did not see a thing! Let's go."

With that, the three friends trundled out of the double doors. At that moment the chimes of Big Ben started.

BONG! BONG! BONG! BONG! BONG! BONG! BONG! BONG! BONG! BONG! BONG! BONG!

Tom listened and counted. Twelve bongs. It was midnight.

The boy was sitting up in his bed. Now it was just him and Sally left in the children's ward. He looked over to her bed. She was asleep, as she had been since Tom arrived in the ward quite a few hours ago.

Despite his swollen head, Tom felt restless. There was no way he wanted to miss out on all the fun. So he took a giant leap into the unknown, and decided to follow them. Tom felt like a super-spy. But the feeling didn't last. As the boy eased himself out of bed, his left foot went straight into the bedpan on the floor.

CLANK!

CLANK!

CLANK!

CHAPTER 8
A PROMISE

CLANK!
CLANK!
CLANK!

Tom couldn't prise his foot out of the bedpan. The boy wanted to shout out in frustration, but knew this would only make matters worse. The last thing he wanted to do was wake up Matron, who was still snoring away in her office. The boy looked over to Sally's bed in the far corner of the ward. She was lying in bed, a glint of light from Big Ben just catching the top of her bald head. Tom didn't want to wake her up either.

At least the bedpan wasn't full, he thought.

As quickly and quietly as he could, Tom reached down and prised his foot from the bedpan. Then he tiptoed out of the children's ward. To his annoyance, his bare feet made squelching noises on the shiny floor.

As his fingers touched the heavy swing doors at the entrance to the ward, he was seconds from freedom. Just then a voice made Tom jump out of his skin.

"So, new boy, where are you going?"

The boy turned round. It was Sally.

"Nowhere," he lied.

"You can't be going nowhere; you must be going somewhere."

"Please just go back to sleep," pleaded Tom. "You will wake up Matron."

"Oh no, they do this every night. That nasty woman won't wake up for hours."

"I really think you should get some rest."

"Boring!"

"It's not boring," replied Tom. "Now come on, go back to sleep."

"No."

"What do you mean 'no'?"

"I mean 'no'. Come on, Tom, take me with you," said Sally.

"No."

"What do you mean 'no'?"

"I mean 'no'."

"Why?" protested the girl.

The reason Tom didn't think Sally should come was that she looked weak. He was worried that she would slow him down. But he didn't want to say that. That would hurt her feelings. So he said something else instead.

"Look, Sally, I am just going to catch up with the

others and tell them they need to come straight back to bed."

"Liar."

"No I'm not!" he said with a little too much gusto, which made him seem like he was lying.

"You are lying. Liar, liar, pants on fire!"

Tom shook his head a little too vigorously.

"I know you must think I'm not going to keep up with you or something," said Sally.

"No!"

"Yes. Come on! Admit it! I'm not stupid!"

No, thought Tom, *this girl is smart. Super smart.* There weren't any girls in Tom's boarding school so he had hardly met any. Tom hadn't thought that girls could be smart. The boy immediately had a feeling that this girl could beat him at everything. Tom didn't like that feeling.

"No, it's not that, honest," lied the boy. Then as he stood there looking at her his curiosity got the better of him. "Sally, can I ask you something?"

"You can ask."

"Why have you got no hair?"

"I decided to shave it all off so I could look exactly like a boiled egg," replied Sally, as quick as a flash.

Tom chuckled. Whatever the girl might have lost, it wasn't her sense of humour.

"Is it because of your illness?"

"Yes and no."

"I don't understand."

"It's actually the treatment that did this."

"The treatment?!" Tom couldn't believe it. If the treatment did this, then what did the illness do? "But you are going to get better, though?"

The girl shrugged. "I don't know." Then she quickly changed the subject. "Do you think you will ever recover from a cricket ball hitting you on the head?!"

Tom chuckled. "I hope not. If I do, then I have to go back to school."

"I wish I could go back to school."

"What?" The boy had never heard another child say such a thing.

"I have been in this place for months now. I miss my school. Even the horrible teachers."

Even though Tom had only just met Sally, it was as if he was talking to an old friend. Then the boy realised he had to leave right now if he was to have a chance of catching up with the others. "I have to go."

"And you definitely aren't going to take me?"

Tom looked at Sally. She looked too unwell to get out of bed, let alone go on some crazy adventure. Tom felt guilty to be leaving her behind, but he felt he had no choice.

"Maybe next time," lied the boy.

Sally smiled. "Look, Tom, I understand. The others have never invited me. You go. But I want you to promise me something."

"What?" he asked.

"I want you to tell me all about the night's adventure when you get back."

"I will," he said.

"Promise?"

"Promise." Tom looked Sally right in the eyes as he said it. He really didn't want to let his new friend down.

Then the boy pushed open the heavy swing doors. Light spilled in from the corridor. Just before he disappeared from sight Sally said, "I hope it's an awfully big adventure."

He smiled at the girl before he pushed the doors open and was swallowed up by the light.

CHAPTER 9
"B" FOR BASEMENT

Pacing down the brightly lit corridor outside the children's ward, it suddenly occurred to Tom that he had absolutely no idea where he was going. His new friend Sally had delayed him somewhat, and now the other three children were long gone.

What's more, **LORD FUNT HOSPITAL** was a spooky place after dark. Distant sounds echoed down the long corridors. The building was tall and wide. There were forty-four floors of wards and operating rooms. There was everything from rooms for delivering babies to a mortuary where people were taken after they died. The hospital was home to hundreds of patients, and nearly as many staff. At midnight all the patients should be fast asleep, but there would still be night staff, including cleaners and security guards, roaming the corridors. If Tom was discovered out of his bed, he would be in big trouble. What's more, he was wearing a pink, frilly nightdress. If anyone was to see him, he would have some serious explaining to do.

Tom looked to the direction signs on the wall, which weren't much help as letters had fallen off.

ENTRANCE & EXIT had become **N IT**.

ACCIDENT & EMERGENCY was now **CIDE R**.

RECEPTION read simply **P O**.

SURGERY now read **SU ER**.

RADIOLOGY had become **RAD LOG**, whatever that was.

ADMINISTRATION was now **MIN T**.

THEATRE was **HEAT**.

CHILDREN'S WARD read simply **WAR**, which might not be such a bad description of what it was like in there.

REHABILITATION had changed into **HAB IT ON**.

PHYSIOTHERAPY had become **H OT HEAP**.

X-RAY had become simply **RAY**, so if you were looking for a man called "Ray" all you had to do was follow the arrow.

There was a sign that read **IF S** which Tom guessed must have been **LIFTS** at some distant point in the hospital's past, and so he followed the arrow.

When he reached the lifts, Tom noticed that the arrow above the large metal shiny doors was descending rapidly. He guessed it might be the three children travelling down. The boy watched as the arrow swung all the way down to "B" for basement.

Tom gulped. It was bound to be dark in the basement. And Tom hated the dark. What's more, the thought of bumping into the porter flashed through his mind. What if Tom felt a hand on his shoulder to stop him and when he looked round it was the terrifying-looking man staring back at him?

For a moment the boy felt like turning back, and then realised that Sally might think he was a scaredy-cat. So, with some hesitation, he pushed the button and waited nervously for the lift to come.

*PIN*G*!*

The doors opened.

*PIN*G*!*

The doors closed.

With his finger trembling, Tom pushed "B" for basement, and the lift trundled down to the darkest depths of the hospital.

With a jolt, the lift stopped.

*PIN*G*!*

The doors opened, and Tom stepped out into the darkness.

The boy was now alone in the basement of **LORD FUNT HOSPITAL**. His bare feet felt

the cold, wet concrete beneath him. Above him on the ceiling was a strip of fluorescent lights, though most had blown, meaning it was all but pitch black down here.

PinG!

Tom jumped. It was just the lift doors closing after him.

The sound of water dripping from pipes echoed along the corridor ahead of him.

Slowly Tom made his way along it. When he came to the end, there were four corridors, two to the left and two to the right. It was a maze down here. The boy looked to see if he could make out any wheelchair tracks on the floor. It was hard to see anything with so little light, so Tom bent down to study the floor. At that moment, a creature brushed past his face.

"Aaarrrggghhh!" His scream echoed down the corridor. At first Tom thought it might have been a rat, but he could just see the creature hopping off. It looked more like a bird, but if it was a bird what was it doing all the way down here?

In the dirt on the floor, Tom could see some tyre marks heading down one of the corridors on the right, so he followed them.

After a few paces, he could feel the stale air in the basement becoming warmer. Just up ahead was a giant furnace where the hospital's waste was being burned. Not far from that, Tom saw a huge basket on wheels. He looked inside. It was full of laundry. Above it was a small hatch. Just then more bed sheets tumbled out of the hatch and fell into the laundry basket. The boy realised that this must be the end of a chute leading down from the wards above.

Every few paces there were doors, and more corridors. Tom followed the tyre tracks as they snaked their way through the basement.

The tracks led on to a corridor that was pitch black.

All the lights in this section of the basement must be broken, thought Tom.

The boy hesitated before going forward. His worst

fear was the dark. Still, it seemed foolish to turn back now. He might be about to find the other children and uncover their secret midnight adventure. Slowly Tom tiptoed forward. Soon it was so dark that he could not see his own hand in front of his face. Now he had to grope along the damp walls to find his way. Just then...

CLANG!

...a deafening noise echoed down the basement corridors. It sounded like a heavy metal door being shut. Tom wondered who else might be down here with him. The porter?

Frozen in fear, the boy stopped dead. He listened. And listened. And listened. But now all he could hear was silence. A deep dread all but swallowed him up. Although he stood still, he felt as if he was running or falling or drowning.

Tom realised that coming down to the basement alone was a terrible mistake. He had to get out of there. Right now. He began to retrace his steps, but in

a panic he lost his way. Soon he was running barefoot down the corridors, the pink, frilly nightdress flapping as he went.

Out of breath, and still feeling woozy from that cricket ball hitting his head, Tom stopped for a moment. Then he felt something grab his shoulder. He turned round. It was a hand.

"Arrrggghhh!" he screamed.

CHAPTER 10

RABBIT-DROPPING ROULETTE

"Wot are you doin' down 'ere?" came an angry voice. It was George. Alongside him were Amber and Robin. Tom turned round and Amber and George immediately collapsed in hysterics.

"Ha ha ha!"

In no time, both were helpless with laughter.

"What's so dreadfully amusing?" asked Robin. "Pray tell!"

"Yes, what is so hilarious?" demanded Tom. He had the distinct feeling they were laughing at him.

"It's your pink, frilly nightdress! Ha ha ha!" laughed Amber.

"It's not mine!" protested Tom.

"Oh, I see," said Robin. "Well, I don't see," he

added, patting the bandages over his eyes, "but you know what I mean."

"Robin, if you could see 'im, you would 'ave a good laugh," added George.

"So how frilly exactly are we talking here?" asked Robin.

"Well…" began Amber. "There are layers of frills like on a wedding cake."

Robin must have created the image in his head because he giggled to himself at the thought. "Oh dear me! Ha ha!"

"**Shut up! The three of you!**" shouted Tom angrily.

"Yes, you boys, no more giggling!" said Amber, even though she was the one who had been giggling the loudest.

"Look, Tom," began George, "we asked you somefink. Wot are you doin' down 'ere?"

"I was following you," replied Tom. "What are you doing down here?"

"We're not saying!" replied Amber. "Now go back to bed, annoying little twit!"

"No. I won't!" replied Tom.

"Get back to bed!" added George.

"NO!" replied Tom defiantly. "I won't!"

"I'd slap you if I could see where you are," fumed Robin. "Count yourself very lucky, Ducky!"

"I'll snitch on you all unless you let me come too!" said Tom.

The other three were stunned into silence.

One thing that was looked down on at Tom's boarding school was snitching. Despite the brutal atmosphere at St Willet's, snitching on other boys to the teachers was forbidden, even if they had…

put trifle in your shoes…

flushed your homework
down the toilet...

buried all your pairs of
underpants...

crammed you into your
own locker...

put a huge hairy spider
in the bottom of your
bed...

made you eat a pongy rugby sock with some cheesy foot shavings sprinkled on top...

painted your nose blue in your sleep...

tied your shoelaces to a tree and left you dangling upside down...

put glue on your tennis racket so it stuck to your hand forever...

 mixed rabbit droppings in with your chocolate drops from the tuck shop. Then forced you to eat them all in a sick game of rabbit-dropping roulette...

So Tom never liked to snitch, or even threaten to snitch, but in this moment he felt he had no other options.

"You better let me come too, or I'll shout and scream and wake up the whole hospital right now!" said Tom.

"I don't think anyone will hear you down here," remarked Robin.

He had a point.

"All right then, I'll take the lift, go up to the ground floor and I'll shout and scream and wake up the whole hospital in just a couple of minutes."

It didn't have quite the same punch, but fortunately

it did the trick. The other three started talking.

"You can't come. Because where we are going is top secret," said Amber.

"What's the secret?" asked Tom.

"We have a secret gang," said Robin.

"Whatever you do, don't tell 'im it's called the Midnight Gang!" said George.

"The Midnight Gang!" exclaimed Tom.

CHAPTER 11
POOP! POOP! AND DOUBLE POOP!

"What do you mean 'don't tell him it's called the Midnight Gang'?!" demanded Amber.

The girl rolled her eyes, and Robin sighed.

"Cool name! I love it! Now please let me join," said Tom.

"No!" said George. "'N' 'O' spells 'no'!"

"Then explain to me why I can't?" protested Tom. The boy desperately wanted to be part of the Midnight Gang, even though he didn't actually have a clue what the Midnight Gang did, because it was secret. What could be more exciting than a gang that was secret? It didn't matter what this secret gang did. All that mattered was that it was secret. Not just secret, but top secret!

Silence greeted Tom's question as the three were stumped for an answer.

"Because it's a secret gang," replied Amber finally. "And it's been secret for years."

"But I already know about it," said Tom. "It's you three and it's called the Midnight Gang!"

"Poop! Poop! Double poop! And triple poop with an extra scoop of poop on top with poop sauce!" said Robin.

"'E's got us!" added George.

Tom smiled smugly to himself.

"No he hasn't," said Amber. "This gang is so much more than that. It's as old as the hospital."

"What do you mean?" asked Tom.

"It was started fifty years ago. Maybe more," replied the girl.

"By who?" asked Tom.

"I can't tell you!" said Amber.

"Spoilsport!" replied Tom.

"Amber can't tell you as she doesn't actually

know," remarked George.

"Thank you for that, George!" said Amber sarcastically.

"No problem," replied George, not detecting the sarcasm.

"Nobody knows who started the Midnight Gang," said Robin. "All we know is that it was a child in this hospital. And it's been passed down by the patients ever since."

"So why can't I join?" said Tom.

"Because not just anybody can join," said Amber. "The Midnight Gang can only survive if it's secret. If someone squealed, it would ruin it for everybody. We don't know if we can trust you yet."

"You can! I swear!" pleaded Tom.

"All right, Tom, listen!" sighed Amber. "You can come with us, but just for tonight. It doesn't mean you are a member of the Midnight Gang. We'll see how you get on. Tonight is strictly a trial period. If you pass the test, then you are in. Do you understand?"

"Yes," replied Tom. "Yes I do. Now, come on, Midnight Gang. Let's have an adventure. Follow me!"

With that, the boy marched off down the corridor.

The other three remained on the spot, shaking their heads.

"Erm, excuse me," said Robin.

"What?" replied Tom, turning back.

"You don't know where you are going."

"Oh yes. Sorry."

"Oh dear, the trial period has already got off to a bad start," said Amber. As she was unable to move her arms, she nodded the direction with her head. "This way, gang! Follow me!"

CHAPTER 12

FOLLOWING THE LEADER

As Amber's arms and legs were in plaster, she was pretty helpless. If she had fallen out of her wheelchair, the girl would have struggled to get up. Most likely she would lie on her back with her arms and legs in the air like an upside-down beetle. However, by sheer force of will, Amber was very much the leader of the Midnight Gang. Down in the hospital basement, she barked orders to George, Robin and the newest member of the gang, Tom.

"Straight ahead! Turn right! Right again! Left again at the end of the corridor."

George had been made to take over pushing Amber's wheelchair after Robin had bashed the girl into too many walls. There were suspicions that Robin had done it on purpose to get out of pushing. Now poor George was covered in sweat and panting like a dog. Pushing the wheelchair was hard work because it had a flat tyre.

"Do you want a go, Tom?" spluttered George as he tried to push the old rusty contraption in a straight line.

"No thank you."

"It's really fun pushin' the wheelchair, ain't it, Robin?" said George.

"Oh yes, George, it's an absolute treat," said Robin, not entirely convincingly.

"Look, Tom," began George, "if you are serious about joinin' our gang, and want this trial period to be a success, then you really need to push Amber's wheelchair, at least for a bit."

Tom sighed. The boy knew he was being tricked into doing it, but could do nothing about it. "All right, all right, I'll do it!"

"Yes!" exclaimed George, punching the air in celebration.

"You boys should be *fighting* for the honour of pushing your leader around," remarked Amber.

"Who said you were the leader?" asked Robin.

"I did!" replied Amber. "Now come on, Tom, let's get going!"

Reluctantly, the boy took the handles and began pushing the wheelchair. Amber was heavier than he had thought, and it was a struggle to get going.

"Faster! Faster!" she ordered.

"Where are we going?" asked Tom.

"Tom, as I said a few moments ago, you are on a trial period in this gang," said Amber. "Our destination is on a strict need-to-know basis, and you do not need to know. Right turn!"

Dutifully, Tom pushed the wheelchair right, and then wheeled Amber to what was, in fact, a dead end.

"STOP!" said Amber. "You've taken me the wrong way!"

"I did exactly as I was told, miss," replied Tom. "I mean… Amber."

"No, 'miss' is fine," said the girl.

"I need to take a break for a moment," announced Tom as he sat down on the floor. The other two boys did the same. "Before we go any further, I need you to explain something to me."

"What?" demanded Amber. The girl was not best pleased. It was clear she wasn't going to be pushed another millimetre unless she gave the boy some proper answers.

"I still don't understand why this child started the secret gang in the first place all those years ago."

"You don't normally get to know all the secrets of the Midnight Gang until you are a full member," replied the girl.

"Please tell 'im, Amber," moaned George. "I can't push any more. I got a stitch."

The girl **harrumphed** at these pathetic boys. "Legend has it that this one particular child was stuck in **LORD FUNT HOSPITAL** for years and years," began Amber.

"Why?" asked Tom.

"I suppose they had something very seriously wrong," replied Amber. "Something more serious than a 'stitch'!"

She shot a look over to George before continuing. "This child was bored. Being ill is boring. Being in hospital is boring. They longed for excitement. So one night, at midnight, so the story goes, they had this brilliant idea to create a secret gang for them and all the other children on the ward."

"But what did this secret gang do?" asked Tom.

"I'm coming to that," replied Amber, "if you would please just let me get a word in edgeways!"

In the darkness of the basement, Tom could just make out George rolling his eyes at him. Amber was certainly a strong  character. No doubt she had put Robin and George in their place many times since they had been admitted to the hospital.

"This one patient thought, why should all the children on the outside have all the fun when they and the other kids couldn't even leave the hospital? Why don't all the kids on the children's ward work together to make one of their dreams come true? Starting every night at midnight."

"Why midnight?"

"Because the grown-ups would not approve.

This child knew that they would do everything in their power to stop the gang if they found out about it. So it had to swing into action only after the grown-ups had all gone to bed. Then, over time, as children left the ward when they recovered from their injuries or illnesses, new children would come. And if the Midnight Gang members thought a new patient could be trusted – *really* trusted – if they were one hundred per cent sure they wouldn't tell the doctors or nurses or their parents or teachers or even their friends outside the hospital, then, and *only* then, would they be invited to join."

"Do you think you would have invited me to join?" asked Tom.

"Probably not," replied Amber curtly.

"Why not?" demanded the boy, more than a little hurt.

"To be honest, you seem a bit of a weed."

"A WEED?!"

"YES! A WEED. Gosh, all that fuss just because you were hit on the head by a tennis ball!"

"It was a cricket ball!" protested Tom.

"Same fing," remarked George.

"No it's not!" exclaimed Tom.

"A cricket ball is much, much heavier!"

"Yes, yes, of course it is!" replied Amber sarcastically. "I imagine they are so heavy a wimp like you would struggle to pick one up!"

The other two boys chuckled as Tom sulked. He knew he was not an Olympic athlete in the making, but he never realised people might think he was a wimp.

"Come on, Tom, don't sulk!" said Amber.

"I suppose the Midnight Gang is nothing more than an idea really," mused Robin. "One that's passed on from child to child."

"Like nits?" asked George unhelpfully.

"Yes, exactly like nits, George!" exclaimed Robin. "You really are a genius. The Midnight Gang is exactly like nits but without the scratchy heads, special shampoo, egg-removing combs and of course the nits themselves."

"All right, all right!" replied George. "We can't all be the Brian of Britain. I mean, Brain of Britain!"

"If the Midnight Gang isn't passed on, then one day it will die out," continued Amber. "We must all remember, even the leader herself, that this is not something that can be done on your own."

"Especially if you need someone to push you around in a wheelchair," remarked Robin.

"The Midnight Gang can only succeed if all the members work together," said Amber.

"But to do what?" asked Tom.

"This is the best bit," whispered Amber. "To bring one of the children's dreams to life!"

"The bigger the dream, the better!" said George.

"I am talking!" said Amber to George.

"Sorry," replied George.

"It's 'sorry, *miss*'," purred Robin.

"So you better start thinking of what your dream is, Tom," said Amber. "Something you've always wanted to do. Have you got one?"

"I wish school dinners were nicer."

"BORING!" said Robin.

"Well, erm, I guess I'd like to be excused from cricket matches from now on..."

"TEDIOUS!"

"Well then, erm, um, I wish I didn't have double Maths on a Wednesday afternoon..."

"Please wake me when he's finished!"

"I don't know! I can't think of anything."

"Come on, Tom," said George. "Surely you can think of some'ink? Thinkin' is not my strong point, but even I thunk of some'ink."

Sadly, though, the boy's mind was blank.

"It seems I was right all along!" exclaimed Amber. "Sorry, Tom, you are just not cut out for the Midnight Gang. Your trial period is now over!"

"No!" protested Tom.

"Yes!" replied Amber.

"Give me another chance! Please? I can think of something!"

"No!" said the girl. "There is no point you being in the Midnight Gang unless you can think of a dream you want to come true. Let's vote! I say we don't let Tom join our gang. Boys? Do you agree?"

"I vote Tom can stay!" said Robin.

"What?" demanded Amber.

"As long as he agrees to push your wheelchair until further notice."

"Yes, if Tom pushes the wheelchair, 'e can stay!" agreed George.

"You two are so annoying!" said Amber. "Right, it looks like you are staying. And pushing!"

"YES!" exclaimed Tom.

"Right! Come on, get up!"

The boy did as he was told.

"Now, spin me round. And push! FAST!"

The boy pushed Amber along the corridor as fast as he could.

"FASTER!" she shouted.

CHAPTER 14

DEEP FREEZE

The four children travelled along corridor after corridor in the basement of **LORD FUNT HOSPITAL**. They passed the boiler room. Tom peered in as he struggled to push Amber in her wheelchair. Inside was a giant water tank the size of a swimming pool. Coming in and out of the tank were huge copper pipes, which **rattled** and **hissed** away.

Next the children passed a dark, dank storeroom. Again Tom peered in. It seemed to be full of nothing more than old junk. A ripped hospital mattress was lying on the floor. The gang pressed on.

Finally, a sign ahead of them read DEEP FREEZE.

"Here we are!" announced Amber.

Tom was only wearing his pink, frilly nightdress.

"You're joking!" he exclaimed.

"What do you mean?" replied Amber.

"We can't go in the deep freeze!" protested the boy.

As they opened the door to what was a giant freezer, which stored tons of hospital food, Amber said, "We're not going into the deep freeze. We are going to the North Pole!"

"The North Pole?" asked Tom. He looked towards Robin and George, but they did not react. "What do you mean we are going to the North Pole?"

"It's always been my dream to be the very first girl to go to the North Pole," said Amber.

"As soon as I am out of hospital, I am going to be a world-famous explorer. I am going to be the first girl to reach

the South Pole too. I want to sail solo around the world. I want to climb the highest mountain, dive down to the very bottom of the sea. I want to have adventures beyond your wildest dreams!"

Tom stood silently listening, wishing he could dream this big. He had always been quiet and even rather timid at school. Tom never wanted to stand out. Now the boy was being asked to reveal his big dream, and to his shame he realised he didn't even have one. Then Tom asked, "Were you exploring when you broke your arms and legs?"

George gave Tom a look, as if to say "don't go there". As for Amber, she looked extremely annoyed at being asked the question.

"If you must know," she began, "it was a mountain-climbing accident."

"Well, that isn't strictly true, is it, dear?" said Robin.

The girl was starting to look uncomfortable. "Well, all right, I was doing mountain-climbing training."

That still sounded impressive to Tom.

"I wouldn't exactly call it mountain-climbing training," said Robin.

"What would you call it then, clever-clogs?" snapped the girl.

"I would call it 'falling off the top bunk'," answered Robin drily.

Tom tried hard not to laugh, but he just couldn't help himself. He burst into helpless laughter. "Ha! Ha! Ha!"

"Ha! Ha! Ha!" laughed George.

Within moments, the rather dry Robin was laughing too. "Ha! Ha! Ha!"

"SILENCE! The lot of you!" screamed Amber.

Seeing how angry this was making the only girl, the boys laughed even more.

"I'm waiting," she said, sounding rather like a teacher.

Eventually the laughter died down, and Amber announced, "Now come on, you silly boys. We are going to be the very first children to reach the North Pole!"

George beckoned Tom to help him, and together the pair slid open the huge metal door to the freezer room.

A blast of arctic air hit the four full in the face.

As the cold air met the warm air, a white mist was formed. At first this mist covered everything. Slowly it cleared, and at last the children saw the most *magnificent sight*.

CHAPTER 15

THE NORTH POLE

The children's faces lit up as they saw the North Pole.

It wasn't the real North Pole, but it was an incredible re-creation of it. Inside the hospital's freezer room, there were inches of snow on the ground. It must have been made from all the flakes of ice that had gathered on the boxes of fish fingers and bags of frozen peas. There were snowdrifts and ice caves and even an igloo. A fan stuck to the ceiling swirled the air around, blowing little pieces of ice about the room. It looked like it was snowing. The snow sparkled in the fluorescent light from the corridor like diamond dust.

" **Wow!** " said Tom.

"It's beautiful," said Amber.

This girl had always seemed to be the toughest of the group, but now Tom could see Amber had tears welling in her eyes.

"Please tell me what you see," said Robin.

In this moment of wonder, the children had quite

134

forgotten that, since the operation on his eyes, Robin
could not see a thing. His bandages had to stay on for
weeks yet.

"It's perfect,"

replied Amber.

"How?" asked Robin.

"Robin, there is snow everywhere," said Tom. "It's falling from the sky."

"I can feel it on my face."

"And there's a snowdrift, and even an igloo," said Tom. "And I don't believe it! Look here, Amber!"

Leaning to the far side of the igloo was a Union Jack flag. It was attached to a wooden pole that looked as if it had been snapped off a building. Perhaps it had been snapped off the side of this very building, the **LORD FUNT HOSPITAL**.

"That must be so you can place it in the snow!" said George. "Like adventurers do. To prove to everyone that you really were 'ere!"

"Place what in the snow?" demanded Robin eagerly.

"A flag!" replied Tom. "Sorry, I should have said."

"Pass it to me!" ordered Amber.

Tom carefully placed the flagpole in her hand. The girl tried to place it down, but as her arms were in casts she couldn't.

"I can't do it!" said Amber, clearly frustrated.

"Let me help!" said Tom.

"NO!" she snapped. "Let's forget the whole thing! This is stupid!"

"It's not stupid," said Tom. "I thought you said the Midnight Gang was all about children working together?"

"It is," replied Amber grumpily.

"Then let me help. In fact, let's all help. Let's all do it together."

"Good idea," said George. He guided Robin's hands to the pole and together they all stuck the end into the deep snow in the middle of the room.

"I hereby declare myself, Amber Florence Harriet Latty, to be the very first girl to reach the North Pole!"

"Hurray!" cheered the boys.

"Thank you, thank you," began Amber grandly. "I really do need to thank a few people."

"Oh, 'ere she goes!" said George.

"This may take some time," hissed Robin to Tom.

"Amber loves making a speech."

"Thank you mostly to myself, without whom none of this would have been possible."

"So humble!" remarked Robin.

"But I would also like to take this opportunity to thank my old friends and new friend in the Midnight Gang."

It might not have been the *real* North Pole, but the look of pride on the girl's face was certainly real.

Tom looked across this mini arctic wasteland. As the mist cleared, the boy saw that the hospital food that was normally stored in the freezer room had been piled up to one side, and covered in ice to disguise it. This begged an important question. Who had done all this?

Just then a shadow passed the gang. Someone or something had moved past the doorway.

"What's that?" asked Tom, a note of terror in his voice.

"What's what?" asked George.

"S-s-*someone's th-th-there*," he spluttered.

"Where?" asked Amber.

"Outside the door," answered Tom.

"It was nothing," said Amber.

"If it was nothing, then go out and have a look," said Tom.

There was silence for a moment.

"Well, I can hardly go out and check in my wheelchair now, can I?" replied Amber.

"I could go out, but the looking part I would find hard," said Robin.

All eyes turned to George. "I would love to go, just as soon as I've finished this tub of ice cream," said George. He had chocolate ice cream around his face, and he dipped his hand into the tub to get another scoop.

Now all eyes turned to Tom.

"I can't go!" he exclaimed.

"Why ever not?" demanded Amber.

The boy looked down to his pink, frilly nightie. "In this?"

"That's hardly a good excuse!" replied Amber. "Girls have to wear nighties. Let's take a vote. All in favour of Tom going to see who it is, put their hands up."

Predictably, the other two boys raised their hands.

"Mine would be raised too if they could. So that's settled then," said the girl grandly. "Off you go, Tom."

"But…" he protested.

"Do you want to be made a permanent member of the Midnight Gang or not?" she asked, already knowing the answer.

"Yes, b-b-but…"

"Then get out there!" she ordered. "Right now!"

The ice underfoot was getting slippery now and Tom nearly fell over with each step. Slowly he reached the doorway to the freezer room. Tom peered out to the left. He couldn't see anything. Then he peered to the right. Out of the shadows came something, the unmistakable figure of… a polar bear.

"Grrr!" it growled.

"Arrrggghh!"

the boy screamed.

CHAPTER 16

POLAR BEAR

It wasn't a real polar bear. It was a man in a polar bear suit. Not the best polar bear suit either. This one was made of cotton wool that looked as if it had been scavenged from the hospital. There were two holes for the eyes, the ears were made of sponges and the nose was made from the end of a stethoscope. The claws were curtain hooks, and the fangs were nothing more than folded pieces of white cardboard from a medicine box.

On seeing the "polar bear" up close, Tom didn't feel so scared any more. He knew it was a person in a suit.

Then the person inside pulled the hood off.

It was the porter.

Man in Polar Bear Suit

Ears made from sponges

Two holes for eyes

Nose made from end of stethoscope

Cotton wool scavenged from the hospital

Fangs made from pieces of white cardboard from a medicine box

Claws made from curtain hooks

On seeing the man's misshapen face, the boy screamed again: "Arrrggghhh!"

"Hello, children!" said the porter cheerfully. "I am so sorry I'm late."

Tom was breathing in and out far too fast now. "W-w-what…?" he panted.

"Slow down, young sir," said the man. "It's only me, the porter."

"So it's you behind this?"

"Yes! It took me weeks to sculpt that arctic wasteland from the ice in the freezer room. Thankfully it hadn't been defrosted for years so there was plenty of 'snow' to play with."

Tom was bemused. He had been told that the Midnight Gang was for kids only, and a secret from grown-ups. Why on earth was this scary-looking man involved?

"Hello, Porter!" said Amber as George and Robin struggled to wheel her to the entrance of the freezer room.

"Good evening, young Miss Amber," replied the man. "I was planning to pop out from behind the igloo dressed as a polar bear and surprise you, but I just couldn't sew on the ears in time."

The man offered up the hood. One of the black sponge ears was dangling by a thread.

"It's brilliant!" exclaimed Amber. "It's your best one ever. I'd hug you if I could."

The porter gently patted her head with his cotton-wool glove. "That is sweet. Thank you, young lady.

The wish to go to the North Pole took rather a lot of thinking on my part."

"I never thought when I was admitted to 'ospital to 'ave my tonsils out that I would end up meetin' a polar bear!" remarked George.

"It's not a real one, George," said Robin.

"Yes, I realised that!" said George. "Soon after 'e took the 'ood off."

"Oh dear," purred Robin.

"But, Porter, why are *you* doing all this?" demanded Tom.

"Me? Oh well, I suppose I've always liked to help out the Midnight Gang, right from the start," replied the man with a glint in his eye. "I've just got to be careful Matron doesn't find out, or I would get fired. On the spot!"

"So why do it?"

"Well, I feel it's worth the risk. I believe that if the patients in this hospital are happy, then there is a much better chance of them getting better."

That makes sense, thought Tom, before asking, "But what if they don't?"

"Even if the patients don't get better, they might *feel* better. And that's worth something."

"It certainly is," agreed Robin.

"I am just a lowly porter, the lowest of the low…" slurred the man.

"You're not the lowest of the low!" interrupted Amber.

"That's kind," he replied.

"There's always the bog cleaner," added George, not entirely helpfully.

"Well, I am sure that makes him feel a whole lot better," said Robin.

"Bog cleaning is important if smelly work, young sir. I never had the chance to go to university and study to be a doctor. That's what I would have really loved to do with my life. I spent a lot of my young life in a hospital, not unlike this one. Trying to straighten this, move that," he said, indicating his misshapen face. "None of it worked. I missed out on a proper education. I would have loved to have gone to school, but I was told it was better I stay at the hospital where I wouldn't frighten the other children."

Suddenly Tom felt a hot surge of guilt. The boy had screamed when he'd seen the porter. Not once, but twice.

"I've been in hospital now for two months with these blasted broken arms and legs of mine," said Amber. "And so many children have come and gone from the ward in that time. So many dreams have come true. And none of us could have done it without you."

The porter looked a little bashful. "Why, thank you, Miss Amber. I have to admit, there have been some absolute beauties, haven't there?"

"Tell me, tell me, tell me!" demanded Tom.

"The Midnight Gang had a thrilling night of racing driving!" began Amber.

"In wheelchairs!" continued the porter. "One young lad called Henry couldn't walk at all. He had been born that way. But young Mr Henry desperately wanted to be a racing driver. So I rewired his electric wheelchair to go super-fast. Seventy miles an hour! He was a blur when he *whizzed* past. Then of course the other children in the ward wanted a go!"

"It wasn't fair!" said George. "Lucky old 'Enry!"

"Lucky?" said Robin. "He couldn't walk!"

"I admit that wasn't so lucky."

"So I found some old rusty wheelchairs that had been left down here to rot," slurred the porter. "I fixed them up with engines that I 'borrowed' from the lawnmowers in the gardener's shed. All the children got a racing number painted on the back of their pyjamas. I used a tea towel as a starter flag, and off they went!"

"We raced round and round the hospital corridors all night!" exclaimed George. "I came third!"

"There were only three children in the race," remarked Amber.

"Yes, but I still came third!"

"I crashed a hundred and three times, but still enjoyed it," added Robin. "Somehow I came in second."

Although the children had started shivering in the freezer room, they couldn't stop sharing their stories of the Midnight Gang's after-dark adventures. "Snow" fell from the ceiling as they told their fantastical stories, every one of them true.

"Then there was a little girl in the ward called Valerie," began Amber. "No more than ten years old. Obsessed with history. Wants to be an archaeologist when she grows up. Her dream was to explore the treasures of ancient Egypt."

"How did you do that?" asked Tom.

"Well, I stole – I mean 'borrowed' – miles of bandage from the pharmacy," said the porter. "Then all the other children wrapped each other in the bandages so they could be Egyptian mummies. I made a pyramid out of empty cardboard boxes, and they all waited inside. When everything was in place, young Valerie found her way into the pyramid and pretended to be the first archaeologist to find the pharaoh's tomb."

"Making my way back to the children's ward, I couldn't see a thing, so I got lost," said Robin. "I wandered into the wrong ward and ended up giving the old dears a fright. They thought a mummy had come back to life! Ha ha!"

"That sounds so exciting," said Tom. "I love the idea of having a spooky adventure like that."

"It's a shame you weren't here with us last Halloween then, young Mr Tom," said the porter.

"What happened then?" asked Amber.

"Yes, none of us four were at the hospital back then," added Robin. "Do tell us!"

"Well, there was a young girl on the ward called Wendy. She was admitted to hospital to have an operation. Wendy hated being in here for so long, as she was missing not just Halloween, when she loved to go out trick or treating, but also her ballroom-dancing classes."

"So what did you do?" asked Tom.

"I thought, why not combine the two? So I organised a ballroom-dancing competition that started at midnight."

"That doesn't sound the least bit **spooky!**" said Amber.

"Well, young Miss Amber, the twist was, all the

children danced with skeletons!"

"Real ones?" asked Tom, rather disturbed.

"No! Of course not! The plastic model ones that the doctors have in their rooms."

"Thank goodness for that!"

"And I let Wendy win, of course."

"At least it wasn't one of the skeletons," said Robin. "That could have been awkward."

"Of course, you three were all here at the hospital when the Midnight Gang went surfing!" prompted the porter.

"Oh yes, a boy called Gerald had lost a leg after a horrible road accident," said Amber.

"That's awful," said Tom.

"What was also awful was that Matron told him he now had absolutely no chance of being a professional surfer."

"Terrible woman!" said Robin.

"But the Midnight Gang were having none of it," continued the girl. "We helped Gerald up on to one of the porter's trolleys. Then working together we raced him up and down the stairs all night like he was surfing the perfect wave!"

"Cool!" said Tom.

"Let's not forget that young fellow who wanted to have tea with the Queen," slurred the porter. "Sandy was his name."

"So how did you do that?" asked Tom.

"I am not sure I looked much like the Queen," said Robin. "I had a shower curtain draped over my shoulders and a bedpan on my head as a crown."

"I was in charge of the Queen's corgis!" announced George proudly.

"How?" asked Tom.

"We snuck around the 'ospital wards at night and collected up the fluffiest slippers. Then we attached 'em to wires on a pole, and I moved 'em around and yapped like a dog."

"It was unbelievably lifelike," said Robin sarcastically.

"Sandy really enjoyed it!" said George.

"He didn't enjoy being hit on the head with your pole!"

"That wasn't my fault!" protested George. "Those corgis were out of control!"

"Quite!" replied Robin.

"Just last week we had a boy on the ward who desperately, desperately wanted to be a comedian," said Amber.

"David was his name, but he just wasn't funny," added Robin. "Painfully unfunny, actually. When telling a joke, David would say the punchline before the set-up. He would say, 'The tomato saw the salad *dressing*. Why did the tomato blush?'"

"What?" asked Tom.

"Oh, it gets worse! 'Is there an owl in there? Who who? Who? Who's there? Knock, knock!'"

"Make it stop!" said Tom.

"This was his best one: 'You're under a vest. Freeze! What did the policeman say to his tummy?'"

"I don't get it," said George.

"It should have been, 'What did the policeman say to his tummy? Freeze! You're under a vest!'" said Amber.

"I still don't get it," replied George.

"Bless poor Mr David," said the porter. "He was blissfully unaware of how unfunny he was. But the boy longed to hear laughter."

"So what did you do?" asked Tom.

"I 'borrowed' a cylinder of laughing gas," began the man.

"What's that?" said Tom.

"Doctors use it to treat pain. But it's called 'laughing gas' because it also makes people laugh. So, without David knowing, I pumped it into a room full of expectant fathers waiting to hear news from the maternity ward. Then I sent young Mr David in there. He told all his back-to-front jokes and – surprise surprise – the expectant fathers all laughed at absolutely everything he said!"

"HA! HA! HA! HA! HA! HA! HA! HA! HA! HA! HA! HA! HA! HA! HA! HA! HA! HA! HA! HA! HA! HA! HA! HA! HA! HA! HA! HA! HA! HA! HA! HA! HA! HA! HA! HA! HA! HA! HA! HA! HA!"

"One of me favourites was when the Midnight Gang swam with dolphins!" remembered George.

"Where was this?" asked Tom.

"In the hospital's water tank, of course!" replied the porter. **"It's huge! The size of a swimming pool!"**

"But what about the dolphins?"

"I pondered 'borrowing' a real one from the aquarium, but thought better of it. Instead, with the help of the children, we painted up some inflatable pillows to look like dolphins. Then I used some ropes and pulleys to pull them along the water. That little patient Mohammed, I think he was only six, but he loved every minute of it!"

"The safari was tops!" said George.

"Yes, that was all for these twins, Hugh and Jack," said the porter. "Hugh had kidney failure and Jack was giving his twin brother one of his kidneys. They were both in hospital for a while because of their operations. So for their Midnight Gang adventure the other children on the ward made animal costumes out of things they found in the hospital. A hose became an elephant's trunk, a furry bath mat a lion's mane, a prosthetic leg a giraffe's neck. We 'borrowed' a mobility scooter. That was their jeep. Then the twins drove around the hospital at night as the other children leaped out at them dressed as the wild animals."

"Marvellous!" said Tom. "Simply marvellous. So have you two boys had your dreams come true yet?"

CHAPTER 18

BA BA BA BOM

"My dream came true just a few nights ago," answered Robin, in the basement of **LORD FUNT HOSPITAL**. "I thought I would set the Midnight Gang an impossible challenge. At school I am on a music scholarship. I always receive top grades in piano and violin, all sorts of instruments really, and want to be a composer one day. I don't like to blow my own trumpet, but I can actually blow my own trumpet. My passion is for classical music. Opera mainly. So my dream was to be the conductor of an entire orchestra."

"This was a challenge," said the porter. "An orchestra might have a hundred musicians. So I had to borrow children from hospitals all over London to help."

"What did they play?" asked Tom.

"Medical instruments!" replied Robin. "And I was the conductor. I chose my favourite piece of music, Beethoven's Fifth Symphony."

BA BA BA BOM! BA BA BA BOM!

"How did it sound?" asked Tom.

"Awful! But it didn't matter how it sounded!" said Robin. "It was how it felt!"

Tom could see the sense of wonder on the boy's face.

"So how *did* it feel?" he asked.

"It's hard to say exactly. But I suppose conducting them felt like I was touching the sky!" replied Robin.

"Wow!" said Tom. He was going to have to think of something extraordinary if he was to top any of these dreams.

"It's my turn next!" said George excitedly. "The next time the Midnight Gang springs into action it will be to make my dream come true."

"Well, just hold on, young Mr George, sir," said the porter. "I am more than a little stuck on this particular wish."

"What is it?" asked Tom.

"He wants to fly," said Amber.

"In a plane?" asked Tom.

"Oh no, no, no! That would be far too simple," replied Robin. "Our George wants to fly like a superhero. Just take off, and *whoosh!* Is it a bird? Is it a plane? No, it's Super-George!"

Tom looked at George. He was a hefty boy. It would be hard to find someone less suitable to take to the skies. It seemed impossible. Perhaps this was a dream too far, even for the mighty Midnight Gang.

The porter was not so easily defeated.

"We'll find a way," he slurred. "Don't you worry, young Mr George, sir, we always find a way. All it takes is imagination. Right, now it's getting late, or early depending on how you look at it. I will clear all this up." The man indicated the North Pole he had created especially for tonight. "Time for you children to go to bed."

The children were all having too much fun.

"**Nooooo!**" they whined.

"**YES!**" replied the porter. "It's way past all your bedtimes."

Reluctantly, the four children shuffled out of the freezer room, and off down the corridor.

"And, young Mr Thomas, sir?" he called out.

"Yes?" replied Tom.

"I am not sure if you enjoy wearing that pink, frilly nightdress…"

"No I don't. Not one bit."

"I thought as much. I don't know why Matron would have given you that to wear. She should have plenty of spare pyjamas in her office."

"Really?" The boy couldn't believe what he was hearing. "Then why would she make me wear this?"

"That lady has darkness in her heart. She enjoys making the children in her care suffer."

"Why?" asked Tom.

"Matron loves being cruel. It must make her feel powerful. That is why she made you wear that nightdress."

"I hate her," said the boy through gritted teeth.

"Don't. That must be what she wants. If you hate her, she's won. And your heart will turn dark too. I know it's hard, but please try not to let her get to you."

"I'll try."

"Good," said the porter. "And in the meantime I'll find you some pyjamas."

"Thank you…" replied Tom. "Sorry, I never really got your name?"

"Just call me 'Porter'. Everyone else does."

It seemed strange calling him that, but there wasn't

time to argue. "Well, thank you, Porter."

"Come on, new boy!" ordered Amber. "Push!"

With a sigh, Tom returned to pushing the wheelchair, and the gang headed in the direction of the lift.

"Freeze! You're under a vest!" said George. **"Ha! Ha! Ha!"**

"What are you on about?" asked Robin.

"I just got the joke!"

"Next time I think it might be quicker to post the punchline to you," joked Robin.

"That would take too long," replied George, without a hint of irony.

CHAPTER 19

POSITIVELY MEDIEVAL

No one dared to speak as the lift made its long journey back up through the hospital to the forty-fourth floor. Amber, George, Robin and the newest member of the Midnight Gang, Tom, all knew they would be in deep trouble if they were discovered out of their beds in the middle of the night. Eagerly, the four children watched the numbers of the floors go up from "B" for basement to...

G, 1, 2, 3...

It was now the early hours of the morning.

4, 5, 6...

LORD FUNT HOSPITAL was still and quiet.

7, 8, 9...

The grown-up patients were all asleep.

10, 11, 12…

A small staff of doctors and nurses were keeping watch over their patients during the night.

13, 14, 15…

PinG!

The children looked at each other in panic. The lift had stopped, and not at the children's ward.

"Oh no! We're busted!" said George.

" *Shush!*" hissed Amber.

Tom was unlucky enough to be standing right next to the lift doors, which began to slide open.

"Say something, Tom!" whispered Amber.

"Me?" protested the boy.

"Yes! You!" she replied.

The lift doors slid open to reveal a hospital cleaning lady. Her name badge read DILLY.

Dilly stood still, her filthy old mop and bucket in hand, a lit cigarette stuck to her bottom lip. The cleaner's mouth fell open in shock, and a long tail of ash fell from the cigarette to the floor.

Dilly stared at the group of children with deep suspicion. At the front was a boy in a pink, frilly nightie, with three children all in nightwear behind him.

"Wot you kids doing out of your beds?" demanded the cleaner. Dilly's voice was deep and gravelly, no doubt from a lifetime of smoking. The cigarette on her lip bounced up and down with each word.

"That's a very good question, madam!" replied Tom, playing for time. "Actually we've been asked by the hospital principal, Sir Quentin Strimmers…"

"Strillers!" hissed Amber.

"…Strillers to check on the quality of the cleaning at the hospital."

"You wot?" demanded Dilly.

"Yes," took over Robin. "We've been inspecting the entire place from top to bottom."

P*IN*G!

The children all looked relieved as the lift doors began to slide shut. But just in time the old lady put her foot in the way and the doors slid open again.

"Why would Sir Quentin ask a bunch of kids to do that?" demanded Dilly.

For a moment the Midnight Gang looked stumped.

All eyes turned to Robin, who was considered the smartest member of the gang.

"The principal wanted children to inspect the cleanliness of the hospital *because*," he began, "as you may have observed, children are shorter than grown-ups and therefore closer to the floor. That makes it easier for us to spot any dust or dirt," he said.

The other three children looked mightily impressed.

"But you've got bandages over your eyes! You can't even see!" said the cleaner.

It was a good point.

"That's where I come in!" said Tom. "I am very much the eyes of the group. And, I must say, that floor is a disgrace."

Dilly was that rare type of cleaner who left everything she touched in a worse state than when she found it. Indeed, she had been cleaning the floor with water that was black with dirt. As a result, there was a dark, dirty smear on the floor where she had just dragged her mop.

"I just cleaned it!" protested Dilly.

"Well, I am very sorry, but it needs doing again," said Tom.

P*IN*G*!*

The lift doors tried to close again.

Once again, there was no escaping.

The cleaner's foot stayed firmly in place in the way of the lift's sliding doors.

A trail of cigarette smoke looped and curled towards the children.

"And I am the nose of the group!" added Amber.

"And, I am sorry to say, there is a toilet on the seventh floor that urgently needs cleaning."

"I just cleaned the bogs there!" complained Dilly.

"Well, you must have missed something," said Amber.

"Or someone's just been and deposited something positively medieval," added Robin.

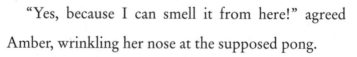

"Yes, because I can smell it from here!" agreed Amber, wrinkling her nose at the supposed pong.

"I can't smell nuffink!" remarked George.

Tom knocked him with his hand to get him to be quiet.

"Now, if you'll please remove your foot from the lift," began Tom, "our hospital inspection committee group thing has to be on its way. We don't want to have to report you to Sir Quentin Strillers, do we?"

The members of the gang all shook their heads and murmured.

"So, if I was you, I would get that toilet on the seventh floor cleaned sharpish!" snapped Amber.

"Yeah, yeah, of course," said the woman, removing her foot. Another ash tail dropped to the floor.

"And one last thing, Dilly," said Robin.

"Yeah?"

"You should quit smoking. There's a rumour going around the hospital that it's bad for you. The next lift will be going down! Thank you so much!" were the boy's parting words.

*PI*N*G!*

CHAPTER 20

THE OATH

Finally the lift doors slid shut, and the four children all breathed sighs of relief. The lift began trundling upwards towards the children's ward. As soon as they were sure they were out of earshot of the cleaning lady, all four burst into fits of laughter.

"HA! HA! HA!"

"Well done, Tom," said Amber. "Cleaning inspectors! Genius! You got us out of that one. I would pat you on the back if I could." With her eyes the girl indicated her broken arms, encased in plaster.

"And I would pat you on the back if I was sure where you were standing," said Robin, a smile breaking out beneath the bandages over his eyes.

"I'll 'ave to do it then!" said George, patting Tom

four times. "That's a pat from each one of us."

"There's three of us!" corrected Amber.

"Sorry, maths was never me strong point," replied George.

"So does that mean I am now a proper member of the Midnight Gang?" asked Tom hopefully. "After tonight's adventures, surely the trial period is now over?"

Silence returned to the trundling lift.

"Please give us a moment to confer," said Amber.

The other three gathered in a corner of the lift and whispered to each other as Tom stood there feeling like a spare part.

"After a meeting of the Midnight Gang," began Amber slowly, "the board of members have decided…"

"It's a yes!" said George.

Amber looked most displeased that the boy had stolen her thunder. "I wanted to make him wait!" she protested.

"THANK YOU!" said Tom. He felt like dancing.

At his boarding school, Tom had always felt like an outsider. He wasn't in the rugby gang. Or the cool gang. Or even the swots' gang. Now he was a member of the most exciting gang in the world. The Midnight Gang. "I am so, so happy."

"Membership fees are one thousand pounds a year payable in cash to me," added Robin.

Tom looked confused for a moment, before Robin's wry smile signalled he was pulling his leg.

"I've never paid it," said a worried George, clearly not getting the joke.

"Well, you can give it to me first thing in the morning," replied Robin.

"But I 'aven't got a thousand quid!" protested George.

"He's joking, you ignoramus!" said Amber. "You do have to swear an oath, though."

"A solemn oath," added Robin. "An oath that pledges allegiance to the Midnight Gang."

"Repeat after me," said Amber. "I do solemnly swear…"

"I do solemnly swear…" began George.

"Not you, George!" said Amber. "You are already a member."

"Oh yes," replied George.

"I do solemnly swear…" repeated Tom.

"That I will always put the needs of my brothers and sisters in the gang over my own…" continued Amber.

"That I will always put the needs of my brothers and sisters in the gang over my own…"

"And keep the secrets of the Midnight Gang forever and a day."

"And keep the secrets of the Midnight Gang forever and a day."

PING!

The lift doors opened at the forty-fourth floor.

"Congratulations!" said Amber. "Tom, you are now officially a member of the Midnight Gang.

CHAPTER 21
A VOICE IN
THE DARKNESS

As soon as the lift doors slid open on to the top floor of the hospital, the four fell silent. Making their way back into the children's ward, they knew they had to be as quiet as possible. Matron would be waking up soon. That is, if she hadn't already.

In the silence of the dead of night, every little noise sounded deafening:

The **clunk** of the tall double doors that opened on to the children's ward.

The **squelch** of Tom's bare feet on the shiny floor.

The *squeak* of Robin's leather slippers every time he took a step.

The **crunch** of the wheelchair's flat tyre.

Tom's **heavy** breathing at having to push Amber.

George **humming** a jaunty tune to himself.

"Shush!" hissed Amber. "We are meant to be being quiet!"

"Sorry!"

It was dark in the children's ward. The only light was either spilling from the matron's office at the end of the ward, or from Big Ben's clock face glowing through the window.

The Midnight Gang was relieved to see that Matron was still asleep in her office, snoring away.

"*ZZZZZ, ZZZZZ, ZZZZZ, ZZZZZZ...*"

Her head was slumped on her desk. A closer inspection from Tom revealed the lady's lips were still smeared with chocolate. Plus a chocolatey puddle of drool had seeped from her mouth on to her desk. Tom smiled to himself at how undignified she looked. Then he tiptoed back to his bed, so as not to wake her up.

"Come on, boys! Help me first!" ordered Amber. The girl instructed the three boys to lift her out of the wheelchair so they could place her in her bed.

However, just as they had hoisted her up a voice came out of the darkness: "Where have you been this time then?"

In shock, the boys dropped Amber on the floor.

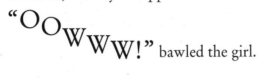 "OOWWWW!" bawled the girl.

CHAPTER 22

SNOTTED

"I asked 'where have you been this time'?"

It was Sally.

The little girl with the pale skin and the bald head was still in her bed in the far corner of the children's ward. Once again, she had been left behind as the other kids had their adventures.

"Nowhere!" answered Amber curtly. She was still smarting after having been dropped on to the floor by the boys as she was being delivered back into her bed.

"You can't have been nowhere," replied Sally. "You must have been somewhere."

"Go back to sleep!" hissed Amber.

"No!" replied Sally. "Tom promised he would tell

me all about the night's adventures. Didn't you, Tom?"

All the children turned towards Tom, who was sliding between the sheets on his bed.

"Well…" said Tom. Inside, the boy was squirming. He knew beyond any doubt that the other three would hate having the secrets of the Midnight Gang divulged to anyone outside the circle of trust. The boy hesitated. He felt torn. Tom had only just sworn an oath to the Midnight Gang, but his heart ached for Sally who they'd left alone in the ward night after night. However, he felt as if he had no choice.

"I didn't promise anything," he replied. Immediately Tom felt a deep pang of shame to have lied.

"You did!" Sally's voice was cracking. The little girl was becoming increasingly upset with them all. "Tonight, just after midnight I asked Tom to take me with him. He said 'no' but I made him promise to tell me all about it afterwards."

"Did you, Tom?" asked George.

Tom hesitated for a moment, before replying. "No."

"YOU DID!" protested Sally.

"I DIDN'T!"

"DID, DID, DID, DID, DID!"

"Please be quiet!" pleaded Amber.

"NO I WON'T!" replied Sally. For such a little girl, she had a big voice. "Not until you tell me what happened tonight. I've watched you creep off after midnight night after night. You need to tell me what you are getting up to!"

"Please, Sally, I beg you, go back to sleep," said Amber. "If Matron finds out, we'll all be in big trouble."

"NOOOO!" shouted back Sally.

The noise must have woken up Matron, as in an instant her snoring stopped.

"ZZZZZ, ZZZzz, ZZ—"

From the other side of the glass that divided the

ward from Matron's office, the children watched as the lady rose unsteadily to her feet. Her hair was sticking up on end and her make-up was smeared across her face. She looked like a clown who had been dragged through a hedge backwards. With a wobble or two, Matron regained her composure and marched through the door into the ward. All the children kept as still as statues in their beds. They didn't dare even breathe, which rather gave the game away that something must be going on.

"I know you nasty little beasts are up to no good," snarled Matron. "And perhaps you got away with it this time, but let me tell you I've got my eyes on each and every one of you."

The lady paced up and down the beds, bringing her face close to each of the children. The smell of her perfume was so strong that when she reached Tom the boy could actually feel it tickling his nose. For a terrifying moment, he thought he would sneeze. Then the feeling passed. Before it came back again with a vengeance.

"AATCHOOOO!" The boy sneezed right in Matron's face.

Tom was so frightened that he didn't dare open his eyes to see the globules of his snot no doubt hanging like icicles from the lady's face. Instead he kept his eyes tightly shut and pretended that his sneeze hadn't woken him up.

Matron was so disgusted by having been snotted on so spectacularly that she retreated at speed into her office. Once inside she put on a pair of transparent rubber gloves, and removed the snot from her face with antiseptic wipe after antiseptic wipe. It was some time before she was satisfied that every speck of snot was removed. Then, to console herself, Matron had another chocolate. Instantly her eyes glazed over and she fell asleep again. Her head thudded on her table as the special snoozy pellet in the chocolates knocked her out.

"ZZZZ, ZZzz, ZZzz, ZZZ."

Snotted

"Well done, new boy!" hissed Amber to Tom. "This is all your fault. Why on earth did you have to promise Sally you would tell her everything?"

"I didn't promise anything." Tom was too deep into his lie to back out now. Each time he lied, the boy felt a little part of him die inside.

"It doesn't matter now!" whispered George. "All that matters is that no one says another word tonight. Matron is on to us! Got it?"

"Yes, we've got it, dear," said Robin. "Now you have to be quiet too!"

"Stop being silly, Robin. Just stop talking and go to sleep!"

"I would love to go to sleep! As soon as you stop telling me to go to sleep and actually be quiet for one moment I will!"

"Will both of you stupid boys shut up and go to sleep right now!" whispered Amber.

After that, none of them said another word.

→ CHAPTER 23 →
DEEP-FRIED OTTER

"Breakfast! Children wake up, wake up, wake up, it's breakfast time!"

This was the cry that woke Tom and all the children in the ward at dawn, just a couple of hours after they had gone to bed.

Matron woke up with a start. A chocolate wrapper was stuck to her forehead.

"What what what?" shouted Matron. It was clear she didn't know if it was day or night, or indeed if she was awake or asleep.

Tootsie was the hospital's dinner lady. She was a pleasing plump woman with a huge Afro hairstyle and the sunniest of smiles. As always, Tootsie was pushing her food trolley.

"Oh no, it's you," snarled Matron as she entered the ward.

"Yes, it's me, Tootsie!" replied the lady brightly. "I hope you haven't been asleep on the job again, Matron!"

Most of the children were sitting up in their beds now. Tootsie always made them smile, especially when she took on their sworn enemy, Matron.

"No, no, no!" lied Matron. "Of course I wasn't asleep."

"What were you doing then?" pressed Tootsie.

"Well, I, er, I was just going through a form on my

desk, and erm… the writing was very small so I had to put my face right next to it! Now get on and serve the children their breakfast this instant!"

"Yes, of course, Matron!"

As Matron busied herself at the mirror, trying to look presentable, Tootsie wheeled her trolley over to Tom's bed.

"Good morning…" Tootsie strained to read the name that had been written on the board above his bed, so she brought down her reading glasses that were nestling on top of her frizzy hair.

"Thomas! Good morning, good morning and good morning to you!"

Tom wasn't sure quite why she had to say "good morning" quite so many times, but he couldn't help smiling. When the lady spoke, it sounded as if she was singing a song.

"Good morning!" said Tom.

"Good morning, good morning and good morning," she replied.

Tom couldn't think of
anything else to say so
once again blurted out,
"Good morning!"

"Good morning!
And what a good
morning it is.
Good morning,
one and all!
Now, Thomas,
what would you
like for breakfast?"

"What have you
got?" asked Tom.

"Everything!"
replied Tootsie.

"Everything?" asked the boy. It was too good
to be true!

"Everything!" she repeated confidently.

All the other children chuckled. This was Tom's

first morning in the hospital and clearly they all knew something he didn't.

The food at Tom's boarding school was terrible. Despite the fees being disgustingly expensive, it seemed as if the food hadn't changed at all since the school was founded hundreds of years ago.

A typical week's menu looked like this:

Monday

Breakfast

Gruel

Lunch

Poached kidneys

Dinner

Calf's-head soup

Tuesday

Breakfast

Pig's trotters on toast

Lunch

Lard sandwiches

Dinner

Stewed lamb's tongue

Wednesday

Breakfast

Leftover stewed lamb's tongue

Lunch

Pigeon soup

Dinner

Boiled eel

Thursday

Breakfast

Offal

Lunch

Braised swan's neck

Dinner

Roast badger with beetroot gravy

Friday

Breakfast

Sparrow's eggs on toast

Lunch

Nettle stew

Dinner

Deep-fried otter

Saturday

Brunch

Toads on toast

Tea

A horse's hoof, with as much

boiled cabbage as you can eat

Dinner

Smoked vole

Sunday

Breakfast

A raw onion

Lunch

Roasted mole with all the trimmings,

followed by bone-marrow jelly

Dinner

Brussels sprout surprise (the

surprise being it was just a

plate of Brussels sprouts)

Of course, Tom was delighted by the prospect of being able to have anything and everything to eat. As he gave his order to Tootsie, his mouth began to water.

"Hot chocolate – oh, with whipped cream on top and marshmallows on the side; a hot buttered croissant – in fact, make that two hot buttered croissants; banana muffins; poached eggs with bacon and sausage – two sausages, please, actually three sausages – brown sauce on the side; and to finish I think I'll have blueberry pancakes with maple syrup, please! Thank you so much! Oh and one more sausage."

This was going to be the best breakfast ever. So why were all the other children on the ward hooting with laughter?

"HA! HA! HA! HA! HA!"

CHAPTER 24
GOODEST MORNING

Tootsie answered Tom with a question. "Toast or cornflakes?"

"But you did say you had 'everything', Tootsie!" replied Tom, bemused.

"Yes, I know I did, Thomas. The truth is we've had a lot of cutbacks here at **LORD FUNT**. The hospital is becoming a sad place now. The new principal has slashed the money for the patients' food. No one wants to stay here a moment longer than they absolutely have to."

"No, I suppose not," replied the boy.

"And I know from working here for thirty years that it makes the patients happy to think they can have absolutely anything their hearts desire for breakfast."

"But they can't," said Tom.

Tootsie shook her head and sighed. This new boy just didn't understand. "As long as the patients only ask for toast or cereal, then they can still believe that they can have anything they want. They'll forget they are in a crummy old hospital that should have been demolished years ago and think they are staying in the Ritz Hotel!"

Tom smiled. Now he understood perfectly, and was determined to play along. "Why, thank you, Tootsie. You know what, I think this morning I'll just have a piece of toast."

"I am all out of toast."

"Cornflakes it is then!" said Tom. "That was my first choice anyway."

The boy didn't mind at all. He rather liked cornflakes.

"I like lashings of milk on my cornflakes," added the boy hopefully.

"Or would you prefer cream?"

"Ooh, yes, please!"

"That's a shame as I don't have any cream."

"Milk is fine then."

"I don't have any milk either. Have you ever had cornflakes with a dash of cold tea?" asked Tootsie.

It wouldn't seem appealing if you had read it on a menu, but the way the lady said it with that musical tone of hers made cornflakes with cold tea sound absolutely scrumptious.

With the flair of a master chef, Tootsie scattered the cornflakes from the box into a chipped green bowl with a single flick of her wrist. Then, from as high as her arm would allow, she tipped the tea urn and poured the dark brown liquid into the bowl. It splashed all over Tom's bedcovers.

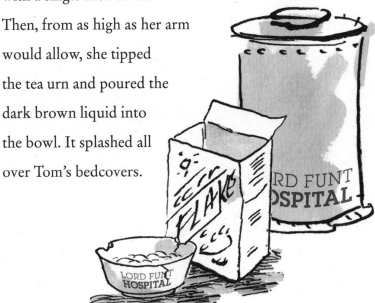

"There we are, Thomas! And I wish you the goodest of mornings! Good morning."

"Good morning."

"Good morning," repeated Tootsie.

"Good morning," said Tom again.

"Good morning."

"Good morning."

If one of them didn't stop, they could go on wishing each other "good morning" until the end of time.

Tom had to step out of the loop, so opted for a "thank you".

"No, thank you," said Tootsie.

"Thank you."

"No, thank you!"

"Thank you."

"No, thank you!"

It was starting again! So the boy nodded and said nothing. Tootsie nodded back and moved on to Amber's bed.

"Good morning, Amber, and what can I get you

this fine morning?" asked the lady.

"Good morning, Tootsie!"

"And good morning to you."

"Let's not do that all morning again, please. Now today for a change I won't have *the freshly squeezed orange juice, blackberries with vanilla yoghurt and honey and the pancakes with nuts, whipped cream and chocolate sauce.*"

"Are you sure?" asked Tootsie.

"Quite sure. I think today what I really fancy is some cornflakes with… let me think… cold tea!"

"Coming right up, Amber!"

As Tom tried gamely to enjoy his "unusual" breakfast, he noticed Tootsie lean in and whisper in Amber's ear.

"Children's footprints and wheelchair-tyre tracks have been found in the freezer room…"

"What?" asked Amber.

"The hospital principal, Sir Mr Strillers, was down there this morning inspecting it."

"Well, it wasn't us!" lied Amber, clearly flustered.

"I never said it was, dearie. But if it wasn't you, who was it?"

"I don't know!" protested the girl.

"Look, I don't know what you children get up to after dark. But, please, from now on be careful."

"Thank you, Tootsie."

"No, thank you, Amber."

"No, thank you."

"No, thank you."

"For goodness' sake, woman! PLEASE can I have my breakfast NOW!" complained Robin bitterly. "I'm STARVING!"

"Yes, of course, Robin!" replied Tootsie as she served him a bowl of dry cornflakes. She had run out of cold tea. George got the same and went into a tremendous SULK.

Next Tootsie moved on to Sally. Under her overalls she had concealed a small white paper bag. "Don't tell the others," whispered Tootsie. "But I bought you an iced bun on the way in to work."

"Thank you so much, Tootsie!" whispered Sally.
"Would you like half, Tom?"

Tom was touched. "No, thank you. You have it.
You need to get your strength up."

"I'll 'ave 'alf!" said George. "In fact, if you want,
I'll 'ave more than 'alf!"

"Let Sally eat her bun!" said Tom.

"It's OK," replied Sally.

George leaped out of his bed as the girl broke it in
two.

"There you—" But before Sally could say "go" he
had taken half of the iced bun out of her hands and
devoured it in one gulp.

"Fanks, Sally," he said. "I'm always 'appy to
'elp."

Tom smiled, then his eyes turned to Matron's office.
She was talking on the telephone, having a heated
conversation with someone. "What was all that about
with Tootsie, Amber?" he asked.

"They know someone's been down in the freezer room," replied the girl.

"How?" asked Tom.

"Footprints. Wheelchair-tyre marks, they're on to us…"

"What are you two conspiring about?" demanded Matron. The children hadn't seen her coming, and she was now looming over their beds.

"Nothing, Matron," replied Amber.

"Yes, absolutely nothing at all," added Tom.

Matron studied their faces for signs of lying. Tom could feel his face glowing bright red.

"I don't believe you!" snarled Matron. "I know you rotten children are up to something!"

CHAPTER 25
THE BOY PROTESTS TOO MUCH

"We ain't done nothin', Matron. If we 'ad done some'ink, which we ain't, then you'd 'ave us bang to rights. But we ain't. All right?" said George.

Matron looked him straight in the eye. The lady was clearly not convinced. "I think the boy protests too much. I have just had the hospital principal on the phone. Sir Quentin Strillers himself. And he was FUMING! Sir Quentin said three small-footed patients had been down in the freezer room in the middle of the

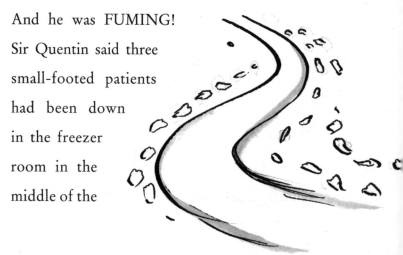

night. And there were wheelchair tracks too. I know it's you. Who else can it be? Now will any of you wicked lot confess?"

All the children fell silent. No one knew how to talk their way out of this.

Then from the corner of the ward came a voice. "I was awake all night, Matron." It was Sally. "And everyone else was asleep the whole time. So it couldn't have been them!"

"Swear it!" demanded Matron.

"I swear, Matron!" Sally put her hand to her heart. "I swear on my pet hamster's life!"

"Hmm," purred Matron. This stopped the lady in her tracks. "Well, you should know I have my eye on every single one of you. Now, Tom…"

"Yes, Matron?" replied the boy, trembling in fear.

"You will be taken down to the X-ray room in five minutes. They need to check on that pathetic little bump on your head. With any luck, you'll be out of this hospital by lunchtime."

"Yes, Matron," replied Tom.

The lady turned on her heels and marched back into her office.

Tom lay back in his bed in sorrow. The last thing he wanted to do was leave his new friends at the hospital. For the first time in his life, Tom felt like he belonged somewhere. His parents travelled abroad so much for his father's work, he felt like he never had a home. And as for his posh boarding school, St Willet's, Tom thought of his time there as a prison sentence. Days and weeks were ticked off in his mind, and the boy knew he was wishing his life away.

Tom felt close to all the children on the ward, but in particular the little girl in the corner. She was special.

"Thank you for getting us out of that one, Sally," said Tom.

"My pleasure," replied the girl.

"I feel bad you swore on your hamster's life."

"It's all right," said the girl. **"I don't have a hamster."**

Tom and Sally laughed.

CHAPTER 26
THE TASTE OF POND

"Wonderful news!" exclaimed Dr Luppers. "There is nothing wrong with you!"

"That's fantastic," replied Tom in the most unconvincing way.

The pair were down in the X-ray room. Doctor Luppers was showing the boy a strange transparent black-and-white photo of his head under a lamp.

"So you can see the bump on your head is this outline here," began the young doctor, "but if we look inside the head here…"

Luppers took out a pencil and pointed to a grey area where the boy's brain was meant to be.

"…then we can't make out any shaded areas at all. So I would say you don't have any internal bleeding."

"Are you sure, Doctor?" pleaded the boy.

"Yes. It's absolutely super news. There's really no point you being here at all."

"No?"

"Yes! It means you can go back to your boarding school immediately."

"Oh!" Tom lowered his head and said nothing.

Luppers looked absolutely baffled that this child was sulking because he could leave. Normally patients wanted to get out of **LORD FUNT HOSPITAL** at the earliest opportunity.

"What's the matter, Tom?" asked the man.

"Nothing. It's just…"

"What?"

"Well, I have made some really good friends on the ward."

"Then make sure you get their addresses before you go, and then they can be pen pals."

Pen pals sounded boring. Tom was yearning for more adventure.

"I will ask Matron to call your headmaster right away to arrange for you to be collected as soon as possible."

Tom realised he had to think fast if he was going to be able to stay with his new friends for another night of adventure.

"I feel very extremely hot, Doctor!" he exclaimed. At his boarding school a high temperature guaranteed you could leave a lesson and have a lie-down in the sick bay. This was a particularly useful way of getting out of double Maths on Wednesday afternoons. Tom had even seen a boy put the end of a thermometer on a blazing hot radiator to fake illness.

"Are you sure?" asked Luppers. He felt the boy's forehead, and wasn't at all convinced.

"Yes! I am burning up, Doctor!" lied the boy. "Hotter than even a particularly hot cup of tea that is too hot to drink!"

Luppers whipped out a thermometer from his pocket, and put it in the boy's mouth. Tom needed a distraction.

"I need a glass of water, Doctor…" he mumbled with the thermometer in his mouth. "Urgently! Or as I am so hot I might spontaneously combust!"

"Oh dear!" replied Luppers, a note of panic in his voice. As he flapped around the X-ray room like a trapped bird, Tom slipped the thermometer out of his mouth and put it next to the fiery-hot light bulb. Immediately the temperature shot up. Then the boy slipped the thermometer back in his mouth, burning his tongue a little in the process.

Luppers returned with a vase of flowers. "I couldn't find a glass. This was the best I could do right now, I am afraid."

Luppers took the thermometer out of the boy's mouth and pulled the flowers out of the vase. Green water with bits of brown bobbing around in it lurked at the bottom.

"Be sure to drink it all!" ordered Luppers.

Reluctantly, the boy started sipping the rank liquid.

"Big gulps, please!" said Luppers. "Every last drop!"

Tom closed his eyes and swigged down the rest of it. It tasted of pond. As he did so, Doctor Luppers studied the temperature in horror.

"Oh no!"

"What?" asked Tom.

"This is the highest temperature ever recorded for a human being!"

Tom worried he might have overdone it. "Do I win a prize, Doctor?" he asked.

"No! But we are going to have to keep you in the hospital until your temperature goes back down to a normal level."

Luppers whipped out a medical form, and began making notes on it.

"Do you have a headache?"

"Ow, yes."

"Fever?"

"Yes! I am burning up!"

"Cold sweats?"

"Yes, suddenly I am freezing."

"Aching joints?"

"Aah, yes."

"Blurred vision?"

"Yes, but, sorry, who is speaking?"

"Dry throat?"

"It's hard to answer my throat is so dry."

"Excessive tiredness?"

"I don't have the energy to answer."

"Hearing problems?"

"Sorry, can you repeat that?"

"Pain when you pass water?"

"Yes, it hurt when I walked past a fish tank."

"Chronic indecisiveness?"

"Yes and no. Doctor, you name it, I've got it!"

Luppers broke out into a sweat. His voice cracked with panic. "Oh my! Oh my, oh my! Oh my, oh my, oh my! It's a miracle you are still alive. We need to do hundreds of tests. Heart tests. Blood tests. Brain tests. Let's just do every test there is. Then we'll get you straight back up to the children's ward!"

Tom didn't say it out loud, but in his head he shouted the most enormous YES!

"Nurse! NURSE!" shouted the doctor, looking as if he was about to faint.

Nurse Meese, who had met Tom on his arrival at the hospital, rushed into the X-ray room.

"What now, Doctor?"

"It is an emergency! This boy needs to do tests. Right now!"

"What tests?"

"All of them! Any you can think of! NOW! NOW! NOW!" spluttered Luppers. "Fetch two trolleys!"

"Why do you need two?" demanded Meese.

"Because I am going to pass out!"

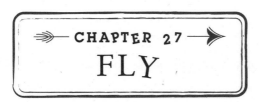

CHAPTER 27
FLY

While waiting for all the results of Doctor Luppers's extremely long list of tests, Tom was under strict bed-rest orders from Matron. The boy's temperature was so high he was forbidden to leave his bed under any circumstances. First, the doctors at **LORD FUNT** had to work out what might be wrong with him. As for Luppers, the newly qualified doctor had been thrown into such a panic he had passed out. In less than a week at the hospital, he had gone from doctor to patient.

As soon as Tom was back in his bed, Sally turned to him and said, "So come on, Tom, tell me…"

"Tell you what?"

"…what you got up to last night."

Tom hesitated. "I'm afraid I can't tell you," he said.

"But you promised."

"I know. I know. I know. Look, I am sorry, Sally, but the others told me it has to be a secret."

"What has to be a secret?"

"The secret thing."

"What is the secret thing?"

"Well, it wouldn't be a secret thing if I told you."

"All right then," replied the girl. It was clear she wasn't giving up. "What were you all doing down in the freezer room last night?"

It became clear Amber had been earwigging, as she joined in the conversation. "For goodness' sake, Sally, the grown-ups are on to us. The principal of the hospital knows something is going on. So, look, the less people who know, the better. If you know everything, you will be in trouble too."

"But I'd love to be in trouble! I hate being left here on my own while you lot go out and have all the fun."

"It's better you don't know," replied Amber.

"But I won't tell anyone," pleaded Sally. "I covered for you all last night, remember?"

"Yes, yes, thank you for that," said Amber. "We may need you to cover for us again tonight."

"We are going out again tonight?" asked Tom. He couldn't believe they would risk it.

"Yes!" cried George from across the children's ward as he tucked into some chocolates. "It's my turn tonight!"

"What are you going to do?" asked Tom.

"Fly?" replied George.

"Oh, please no!" said Robin.

"What do you mean 'oh, please no'?!" demanded George.

Matron must have heard the raised voices, because she dashed out of her office.

"What's all this now?" she demanded.

"Nothing, Matron!" replied Amber. "Nothing at all."

"Really? Nothing indeed. It seems I have a ward of nasty little liars. Now, my shift is finishing soon. Nurse Meese will be here in a moment. She will be in charge of the children's ward until nightfall. Then I shall return. If Nurse Meese has to report bad behaviour from any of you, I will have all of you thrown out of here and moved to separate hospitals. Do you understand me?"

"Yes, Matron," the children all said together.

"Good," purred Matron. "Sally, you will be going down for your treatment soon."

"Do I have to?" asked the girl.

"**Stupid child!**" snapped Matron. "Yes, of course you do! What do you think you are here for? To have fun?"

"No, Matron," replied the girl.

At that moment the tall doors at the end of the ward

swung open with force. Nurse Meese entered and said, "Morning, Matron. Morning, kiddies."

"Good morning, Nurse Meese," said the children in unison.

"Morning, Meese," said Matron.

"How is that temperature of yours, Thomas?" asked the nurse. By her tone, it sounded as if she suspected the boy was faking it. She was much more experienced than the new boy Luppers, and so harder to fool.

"Still very incredibly high, Nurse," replied Tom.

"That boy is not to leave his bed," said Matron. "Under any circumstances!"

"Yes, Matron. You can trust me. I will make sure of that," said Meese as she eyed the boy suspiciously.

CHAPTER 28

THE IMPOSSIBLE DREAM

Later that afternoon, the Midnight Gang began planning the night's adventure. George's dream was to fly. This would take some thinking. Especially as it seemed the top brass at the hospital were on to them.

With Sally downstairs receiving her special treatment, and Nurse Meese sitting in Matron's office, the children set to work.

The children's ward of **LORD FUNT HOSPITAL** had a few tatty old board games. There was a Snakes and Ladders set that had no dice, a jigsaw of a cute white kitten playing with some balloons that had a number of pieces missing, and a game of Operation with no batteries so the patient's nose never lit up red.

Tom, Amber, George and Robin all pretended to work on the jigsaw together as they talked in hushed tones about tonight's adventure.

"Maybe we could make a glider out of sheets and curtain poles?" suggested Robin. "The porter can help us put everything together."

"But where would we fly it?" replied Amber. "There's nowhere high enough in the hospital."

"There's the stairwell," said Robin. "This hospital goes up forty-four floors. So it must be a long drop."

"Erm, excuse me," said George, "I wanna fly, not die!"

"You would have a glider," replied Robin.

"Well, I would 'ave some sheets and poles tied together. That's not the same fing!" said George a little too loudly.

All eyes turned to the office, but Nurse Meese was busy with her paperwork.

"Well, maybe you shouldn't have such an impossible dream!" remarked Amber.

"But it's always been my dream. I 'ate bein' 'eavy like this." George slapped his big stomach and it wobbled like jelly for a few seconds. "I want to feel

what it's like to be as light as air."

Tom had been listening to everything, and searching his mind for an answer. As he placed a jigsaw piece down on the tray table in front of him, he realised the answer was staring them all in the face.

"Balloons!" he said.

"Wot?" asked George.

"Let's not go down, let's go up!" said Tom.

"Please would you be so kind as to explain, new boy!" said Amber.

"You know at a

birthday party when you sometimes have those special balloons that float?" began Tom, his words tumbling out in excitement. The other children all nodded in agreement.

"Well, if we could get our hands on enough of them, then George could start at the bottom of the stairwell and float up!"

George smiled. "Tom! I love it!"

"Are there enough balloons in Britain?" asked Robin.

"Very funny!" replied George.

"I bet there are enough dotted around this hospital," replied Tom. "Patients often have them tied to their beds. There's one right there!"

With his eyes, Tom indicated over to Sally's bed. One lonely balloon with "Get Well Soon" printed on it was tied on to her headboard. It was floating in the air just shy of the ceiling.

"What a brilliant idea of mine!" said Amber. The girl obviously wanted to be back in charge again, and didn't like this new boy stealing her thunder.

"What?" protested Tom.

"I was about to suggest balloons just before you did," she fibbed.

"Of course you were!" said Tom.

"Come on, ladies! Let's not fall out!" joked Robin.

"I bet there are 'undreds of those balloons in this 'ospital," said George in a rush of excitement. "There's loads for sale in the gift shop on the ground floor. I often sneak down there to buy a chocolate bar or two. All we need to do is steal 'em!"

"Borrow them!" said Tom.

"Yes, the boy is right," added Robin. "'Borrow' them. It's a much nicer word than 'steal'."

"As soon as we 'ave 'borrowed' enough," said George, "I'll be able to fly right up to the top of the stairwell. I will finally take to the air!"

George's face was glowing with joy at the thought. The plan was so simple it was brilliant. "Let's tell our mate Porter!"

The Impossible Dream

All the children had to do now was steal hundreds upon hundreds of balloons from all over the hospital. Without getting caught.

CHAPTER 29

BALLOONS, BALLOONS AND MORE BALLOONS

Once darkness fell, the mischief began.

Matron had arrived back at nightfall for her shift. The children had seemingly been on their best behaviour all day, working on a jigsaw, and so Nurse Meese had nothing to report.

Matron had not been back on the children's ward for long when she had confiscated another of George's secret tins of chocolates that his newsagent Raj had sent him. Then she retreated to her office to scoff her favourite purple-wrapped ones. Once again, George had pushed one of his special snoozy pellets in each one. Within minutes Matron was snoring as loudly as an elephant.

"ZZZZ-ZZZZ, ZZZZ-ZZZZ-ZZZZ-ZZZZ!"

That part of the plan always worked perfectly.

Now the Midnight Gang had to get their hands on every balloon in the hospital. They needed balloons, balloons and more balloons.

The children divided themselves into three teams.

Team One was Amber and Robin. They would help each other and cover everywhere from the children's ward at the very top of **LORD FUNT HOSPITAL** down to floor thirty.

Team Two was George. He would work alone and take floors twenty-nine down to sixteen.

Team Three was Tom and the porter. They would have the most dangerous task, collecting all the balloons from the fifteenth floor down to the ground floor, including the gift shop, which had big bunches of helium-filled balloons on sale.

As the nearby Big Ben chimed twelve times for midnight, the boys crept out of their beds to lift Amber out of hers and lower her into her wheelchair. Tom and George tiptoed out of the ward through the double doors.

"Our first balloon to swipe is just to your left," hissed Amber to Robin.

Although Robin couldn't see, he knew she meant the one tied to Sally's bed.

"Amber! Please!" whispered Robin.

"What?" she protested.

"I know you have elected yourself leader of the gang, but we can't take Sally's balloon!"

"Why not?"

"Because we can't!"

"Robin! We need as many as we can get. Now wheel me over to her bed at once!"

"No!"

"At once!"

Out of the darkness came a voice. "It's all right. You can take it."

"Sally?" asked Amber.

"Yes. I don't mind. What do you need it for? Another adventure?"

Robin wheeled Amber over to the little girl's bed.

Sally looked weaker than ever. Even though it helped make her better, Sally's treatment always made her feel worse for a while. Tonight she looked particularly pale.

"We were only going to 'borrow' the balloon," replied Amber.

"Take it. I don't need it. All it does is bob around all day."

"Well, thank you, Sally, that is most kind of you," said Robin. "Now just guide my hand over to the string so I can untie it."

As Amber looked on, Sally held the boy's hand and led it to the string. But she didn't let go.

"Take me with you," said Sally.

Robin began untying the balloon.

"I am so sorry, Sally," began Amber, "but I am afraid you can't come with us."

"Why not?" asked the girl.

"Look, if you must know, we have a secret gang, but it's completely full and we aren't looking for any new members right now."

"But you just let Tom join!" protested Sally. The girl had a point. "He had only been in the hospital for one night and he got to come on an adventure with you."

"Well, you see..." Amber was scrabbling for her words. "That was different."

"Why?" demanded the girl.

"Because... because... because if you must know, Sally, you would slow us all down!" answered Amber.

At hearing this, a single tear rolled down Sally's cheek.

The sight of this made Amber want to cry too. It was sad enough looking at Sally, with her bald head and pale skin that made her look like a piece of porcelain. Like a piece of porcelain, Sally looked as if she needed to be handled with care.

"Sorry," said Amber. "I would reach out to hug you, but as you can see it's impossible with my arms in plaster."

Robin, whose sarcastic comments concealed a

more caring side, stroked Sally's head.

"I understand," said Sally. "I am used to being left out of everything. Ever since they said I had this illness, I was told I couldn't do this or that. But it's so boring having to lie in bed all day. I want to be a little girl again and have fun." She sighed. "Please take my balloon, and have the most brilliant adventure tonight, whatever it is you are going to do. But promise me something…"

"Anything," replied Amber.

"…Take me on your next adventure. Please? I'll be strong enough then. I just know I will. I promise."

Amber smiled, but said nothing. She didn't want to give the girl false hope. Then she ordered Robin to get moving.

"Chop chop, Robin! Come on! We need to get going."

"I'm sorry, Sally," said Robin.

Then, with the little girl's balloon in hand, he pushed Amber's wheelchair through the heavy swing doors.

"OW!" cried Amber, her bandaged legs knocking hard against the doors.

"Sorry!" cried Robin.

Sally chuckled to herself as she watched them go.

"Good luck, gang," she said.

CHAPTER 30

AN OLD FRIEND

Meanwhile Team Two, or "George" as he was known, was busy working through his floors. The boy was crawling around the wards on his hands and knees.

George already had quite a haul of balloons that he had "borrowed" from the patients. All said "Get Well Soon" on them, and had probably been given by a loved one. However, George was too excited to feel any guilt. With every balloon, he was getting closer to his dream of flight. The tricky part was holding on to his bunch of balloons while untying others. Soon George had large bunches of balloons tied to both arms and both legs. Yet still he needed more and more and more.

Just as he was crawling out of the final ward on the twenty-ninth floor a voice called out...

"George?"

The boy would know that voice anywhere. It was the voice of his local newsagent.

"Raj?"

"Yes! It's me, Raj. George! My favourite customer! Did you receive the tins of chocolates I sent you?"

"Yes, thanks a bundle!"

"I was worried about you when I heard you had to have your tonsils out."

"I am feelin' much weller now, thanks, Raj. Those choccies 'ave really cheered me up."

The newsagent smiled. "Good, good, good and again good! They were the absolute best tins of chocolates in my shop. Left over from a few Christmases ago. Only a few years out of date."

"Still, it was nice of you, mate."

"Come back soon, George. Takings are down since you haven't been coming in."

"I will!" replied the boy with a chuckle. "What are you doin' 'ere in the 'ospital?"

The newsagent was sitting up in bed in his pyjamas with his fingers bandaged. "Two nights ago I was involved in a very serious stapler accident. I was in my shop stapling some prices to products. I had some very special offers on. One hundred pencils for the price of ninety-nine. Buy a ton of toffees – get one toffee absolutely free. Second-hand birthday cards with the names Tipp-exed out, half price. And, somehow, I managed to staple my fingers together."

"Ouch!" replied George. "That sounds well painful."

"It was," said Raj mournfully. "I would not advise stapling your own fingers together to anyone!"

"I will remember that, mate. Well, I would love to stay and 'ave a natter but…"

George was just beginning to scuttle out, when Raj called him back.

"George?"

"Yeah, mate?"

"What are you doing with all those balloons?"

"Erm, um…" George spluttered. "They are my balloons, ain't they?"

"Really?"

"Yeah."

"All of them?"

"Yeah, mate."

The newsagent did not look at all convinced.

"That one says 'Get Well Soon, Mum'," he said.

"I fink there was a mix-up at the balloon shop."

"Mmm!" replied Raj, unconvinced. "But what are your balloons all doing down here? The children's ward is on the very top floor of the hospital."

George thought for a moment. "They floated down, didn't they?" he replied.

"But these balloons only float up?"

"Well, I can't stay natterin' all night," said George, turning to go.

"Oh, my favourite customer, please could you do your favourite newsagent a favour?" he asked.

"Sorry, mate, I gotta go."

"It will only take a moment of your time, thank you kindly, George, my favourite customer."

"Wot is it then?" sighed the boy.

"Well, the food in this hospital has been shocking. This very nice lady called Tootsie comes round with her trolley, promising she has everything on it. You ask for something and then it turns out she's only got a cheese triangle and a sachet of brown sauce."

"Yeah, I know. You and I both love our grub."

"We certainly do!" said Raj, slapping his tummy. "So, as a thank-you for the chocolates, please could you get your favourite newsagent a takeaway? I would call for one myself, but since the stapling incident I can't use my fingers!"

With that, Raj displayed his bandaged fingers.

"Can I come back later, mate?"

"I worry I may have wasted away by then," he said, slapping his large round tummy again, which looked big enough to fit a beach ball inside. "So please can you take my order now?"

"Will I need to write it down?"

"No no no, it's just a couple of things. It will be very easy to remember."

"OK," replied the boy. "Off you go…"

"Thank you. So I would like an onion bhaji, samosa, chicken jalfrezi, aloo chaat, tandoori king prawn masala, poppadoms—"

"You are doin' me nut in! I can't remember all that…" interrupted the boy. However, Raj's eyes were

glowing and his mouth was watering at the thought of all this delicious food.

"No, no, no, you'll be able to remember it. Just a couple more... vegetable balti, peshwari naan, chapati, aloo gobi, matar paneer, tarka dhal..."

"I need a pen and paper!" said George, panicking.

"Poppadoms..."

"You said poppadoms already, mate!"

"Yes, I know, I want two portions of poppadoms! Mango chutney, paneer masala, pilau rice, bharta, chana aloo, lamb rogan josh. I think that's all. Did I say poppadoms?"

"YEAH! TWICE!"

"Good, you can never have enough poppadoms. In fact, make that three portions of poppadoms. Right, now just recite that back to me!"

When George finally escaped from Raj's ward, he realised the best plan was just to order every single item on the menu of the nearest Indian restaurant. Plus to ask for four portions of poppadoms in case three didn't turn out to be quite enough.

Now out in the corridor, George called the lift to take him down to the ground floor. There he would meet the rest of the gang at the bottom of the impossibly tall stairwell.

PING!

The lift doors opened. Inside was the old

chain-smoking cleaner who the Midnight Gang had met only last night. Dilly was holding on to the handle of a floor-polishing machine, and as always had a burning cigarette stuck to her bottom lip. Her mouth opened at the shock of seeing George with a hundred balloons tied on to his arms and legs.

The boy had so many that he was actually beginning to feel a little lighter. George's head was just visible, nestling between the balloons.

"Wot are you up to now?" she demanded. A trail of ash fell from her cigarette to the floor.

"Oh, 'ello again!" replied George brightly. "The cleanliness inspection last night was all tickety-boo, so keep up the great work. Although we did find some cigarette ash on the floor. We weren't sure if that was you…"

"Wot are you doing with all those blasted balloons?" asked Dilly. "I got a good mind to pop 'em all with me fag!"

The "floated down" excuse hadn't worked that well on Raj, so George tried another explanation.

"I am just deliverin' these to an incredibly popular patient. He actually gets sent thousands of balloons daily. So don't worry – I'll get the next lift!"

*PI*N*G!*

The doors slid shut on her.

George stamped the floor in frustration. He had been seen by a member of hospital staff out of bed in the middle of the night. The Midnight Gang would now have to move fast if George was to realise his dream.

CHAPTER 31
THE WORLD'S OLDEST CHILD

Meanwhile, a few floors below, Team Three was sweeping through the wards of sleeping patients, on the lookout for balloons. Tom and the porter both found it hard work, crawling along the floor on their hands and knees, trying not to be seen. What made it even more difficult is that they both had dozens of balloons tied to them.

It was way past midnight now and all that could be heard was the snoring of the patients, many of them old.

"ZZZzz, ZZZzz, ZZZzz, ZZZZz"

The nurses were at their stations, but with nothing much for them to do in the middle of the night some had dozed off, while others were reading books. Just as Tom and the porter were crawling out of the big swing doors at the end of a ward, they heard an old lady call after them, "Ooh my! What beautiful balloons! Are they for me?"

Tom looked to the porter, who put his finger up to his lips to signal to be as quiet as possible.

"I said, are they for me? I do so love balloons." The voice was louder this time. It couldn't be ignored. There was a chance the nurses who were napping at their station just a few paces away would wake up if the old lady said another word.

Tom looked up. An impossibly elderly woman was sitting up in her bed. Her face was wrinkled and her hair white as snow. Unlike most of the other patients, she didn't have any cards or flowers by her bed. Her table was completely bare, aside from a jug of water and a plastic cup.

"Come on!" said Tom to the porter. The boy wanted to press on, but the porter looked torn.

The man shook his head. "Mr Tom, sir, we can't just ignore her."

"I have never seen such beautiful balloons in all my days. I love them!" said the old lady. "Who sent them to me? Was it Father?"

The lady looked in her nineties, maybe even older. It was as if the years had shrunk her, like a piece of fruit left out in the sun. Tom realised it wasn't just the old lady's body that had weakened. Her mind must have done too if she thought her father was still alive. It was impossible.

Tom was completely lost as to what to say or do.

As he rose to his feet, the balloons bouncing around him, he whispered to the porter, "Her father can't still be alive, surely?"

"No. Of course not," whispered back the porter. "Nelly here is ninety-nine, and has no family left alive."

"What shall we do about the balloons?" asked Tom.

"Nelly thinks she is still a little girl. So we must play along. Let me."

The porter turned to the old lady. "Yes, Nelly, your father sent you this." He handed the old lady the balloon that was closest to her. It was one he had swiped several beds earlier. It was a little deflated, and had "I Love You, Grandad" written on it. Not that Nelly seemed to mind. Her face lit up as she held the string.

"Oh, I love this one. It's absolutely beautiful!" she cooed. "And you are beautiful for delivering it to me."

Tom looked to the porter. The boy imagined the man had never been called beautiful before.

"Did Father have a message for me? When he might be picking me up?"

As the porter was lost for words, Tom stepped in.

"Soon, Nelly," the boy said. "You'll be seeing him very soon."

"Really?"

"Yes. Really," replied Tom.

"Oh, goody goody!" The old lady smiled and the years melted away. It was as if she really was a little girl again.

"We have to go," said Tom.

"Are you delivering balloons to the other children like me in the hospital today?" she asked.

"Yes," said Tom, his voice cracking with emotion. "That's exactly what we are doing."

"Splendid!" she replied. "You have so many – be

careful you don't take off! Ha! Ha!"

Tom and the porter shared a look. She was one step ahead of them.

"We must go!" said the porter.

"Do come back and see me again soon," said the lady, her eyes marvelling at her new toy.

The pair scurried out through the tall double doors, the clouds of balloons following in their wake.

CHAPTER 32

BALLOON BURGLARS

The time was now 2am, and the hospital gift shop had been shut for hours. Tom pushed his face up against the glass. Inside were huge bunches of balloons for sale.

They were all freshly inflated and nestling against the ceiling like a ginormous bouquet of flowers.

"That's what we need to get our hands on, young Mr Tom, sir," said the porter.

"But how are we going to get into the shop?" asked the boy. "It's locked!"

"I don't know," replied the man. "But we must. Time is marching on and we can't let young Mr George down. This is his big night."

The sound of some kind of machine droning could be heard at the far end of the corridor.

WHIRRR.

It was Dilly the cleaning lady.

Tom and the porter looked at each other in a panic, and hid behind the wall of the gift shop.

Dilly slowly made her way along the corridor, swinging the polisher across the floor and dropping cigarette ash as she went. Then she turned the machine off, took out a big bunch of keys and unlocked the door to the shop.

Next the cleaner turned the machine on again.

WHIRRR.

Dilly began polishing the floor inside the gift shop, again dropping cigarette ash everywhere.

The balloon burglars smiled to each other. This was their chance.

The drone of the machine was so loud it covered the noise of their footsteps as they entered the shop.

WHIRRR.

With Dilly's back turned, they rushed over to the far corner of the shop where the balloons were nestling. The pair grabbed as many bunches as they could, and added them to their already impressive haul.

WHIRRR.

However, just as they had reached the door to the gift shop, the sound of the machine stopped dead.

Tom didn't dare look back.

"Oi!" shouted Dilly. "Wot is it with balloons tonight? You gotta tell me what the heck you two are up to! Now!"

"Oh! Hello, young Miss Dilly!" slurred the porter.

"It's you!" the cleaning lady replied. "I should have known. You are always lurking around the hospital, up to no good."

"Not at all!" replied the porter, trying hard to rearrange his misshapen face to make a smile. "Young Mr Tom and myself are just taking all these balloons up to the children's ward."

"Whatever for?" demanded the cleaner.

"I am running a balloon-animal-making competition!" said the porter.

"In the middle of the night?!"

"We are mainly making badgers and owls, and as I am sure you know they are nocturnal creatures and so only come out at night," added Tom.

"I don't believe a word of it! You're both lying. All you rotten kids are up to no good. You've got no right to steal those balloons. I'm reporting you to hospital security right now!"

"Oh no! What shall we do?" pleaded Tom.

"Leg it!" replied the porter.

The pair raced out of the shop, the porter dragging his withered leg behind him.

Spotting that the bunch of keys was dangling

from the door, Tom turned the key, locking the poor cleaner in.

Furious, Dilly banged on the glass doors.

THUD!

THUD!

THUD!

THUD!

"LET

ME

OUT!"

she shouted as more cigarette ash dropped from her mouth.

However, the pair of balloon burglars was already halfway down the corridor, trailing hundreds of balloons behind them.

"YOU ARE LATE!" shouted Amber as Tom and the porter finally arrived. George was standing beside her, not looking best pleased either. All three teams were now gathered at the bottom of the tall stairwell, which

stretched from the very bottom of the hospital to the very top. Everyone was holding huge bunches of balloons. Of course, being the unofficial leader of the Midnight Gang, Amber had to have the largest number of balloons. It looked like two or three hundred. All of Amber's balloons were tied to her wheelchair. There were so many that she was hovering off the ground ever so slightly. One more balloon and she might just have taken off. It was clear that she and Robin had been very busy in their attempt to make George's dream come true.

"Sorry!" said Tom as he and the porter arrived. Standing at the bottom of the stairwell, Tom finally had a sense of how incredibly tall **LORD FUNT HOSPITAL** was. Looking up, he felt dizzy. Tom had never been in a building so tall before. A giant staircase led all the way down from the very top of the hospital. There must have been a thousand steps in all, and the ceiling was a huge glass skylight. Through that Tom could see stars twinkling in the night sky.

Everyone's faces were glowing with the excitement. To be out of their beds in the dead of night was always a thrill.

"OK, everyone. Give me your balloons!" announced George. He couldn't wait a moment longer.

"Patience, young Mr George, sir!" said the porter. "This is a delicate operation. We need to get the number of balloons just right. If you take all the balloons now, you could zoom all the way up there like a rocket."

"That's exactly what I want!" protested the boy.

"Chance would be a fine thing," remarked Robin.

If you are thinking of making your pet fly.* here is the number of balloons you will need...

A gerbil: 7 balloons.

A hamster: 12 balloons.

*Please ask the pet first, as some do like to stay on the ground.

A rabbit: 31 balloons.

A tortoise: 39 balloons.

A cat: 47 balloons.

A dog: 58 balloons.

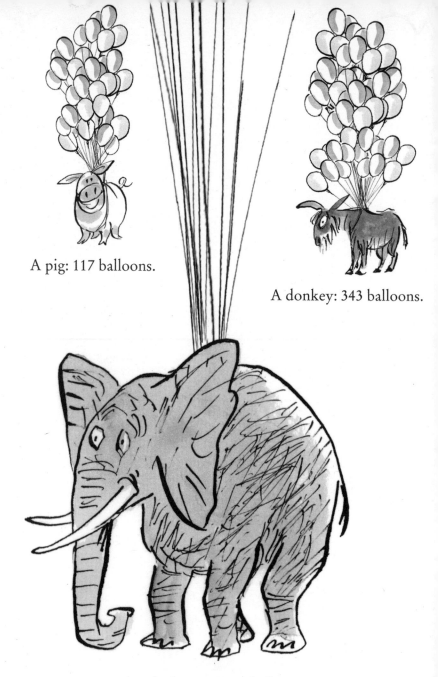

A pig: 117 balloons.

A donkey: 343 balloons.

An elephant: 97,282 balloons.

A blue whale: 3,985,422 balloons.

"I am already floating! Look!" said Amber. The girl was hovering a few centimetres off the ground. "And that is with the weight of the wheelchair!"

"All right! All right!" said George impatiently.
"Just tell me what to do!"

"First someone needs to go to the very top of the

stairs to take just one balloon off George so that when he has floated up he can safely float back down," said the porter. "Hands up if you want to volunteer!"

Needless to say, none of the Midnight Gang wanted to climb a thousand stairs.

Without thinking, Tom lifted his hand to pick his nose.

"Thank you, young Thomas, sir," said the porter.

"But—" protested Tom.

"Very noble of you. Off you go!"

Reluctantly, Tom began ascending the stairs. At first he stomped to show his annoyance, but that soon became exhausting so he stopped and simply climbed them. Tom could hear everything that was going on below as the voices echoed up the stairwell.

As usual, the porter organised everything for the children. He began gathering the balloons bunch by bunch, before handing them over to George.

In no time, the boy was starting to feel weightless, his feet skimming the ground.

"We need to be very careful now," said the porter. "One balloon at a time."

Finally, Tom had reached the very top of the staircase. He was now completely out of breath. Tom was not sporty at all and to him this was like scaling Mount Everest. The boy looked down and felt a hundred times dizzier than when he had looked up. It was as if he was going to fall, even though with the handrail there was no way he could.

George was now floating a few centimetres off the ground. One or two more balloons and he would be soaring through the air.

"Are you ready up there, Mr Thomas, sir?" called the porter.

"Ready!" Tom shouted back down, though for a

moment he had forgotten what he had gone all that way up there to do. "Take a balloon off George so he can safely float back down again," he muttered to himself, suddenly remembering.

The porter held one balloon in his hand to George's hundreds. "I am sure this is the one that will finally make you fly. Are you ready?"

"Ready!" replied George.

The porter looked over at Amber and Robin. "All together now, let's make it like the launch of a space rocket... **Ten, nine, eight...**"

The Midnight Gang all began counting down together.

"Seven, six, five, four, three, two..."

But before they could say **"one"** the impossibly old lady, Nelly, waltzed into the bottom of the stairwell clutching her balloon.

"Oh, hello again," she said brightly. "As much as I love this balloon you gave me, I wondered if I could swap it for a pink one."

Nelly reached out and grabbed the huge bunch of balloons George was holding.

As soon as she did so, her little body shot up through the air faster than a rocket.

ZOOM!

Tom desperately tried to catch the little old lady as she flew past, but she was going way too fast. The old lady was much lighter than George, and the helium in the balloons made her zoom up the stairwell at terrific speed.

CRASH!!

Glass fell from the skylight as Nelly smashed through it.

Those down below leaped out of the way to avoid the sharp shards of falling glass. The shards hit the ground with a gigantic…

S_M_A_SH!

"*Yippee!*" shouted the
old lady with joy as she
disappeared off into the
starry sky.

"Not fair!"

shouted George.

From the top of the stairwell, Tom could see Nelly sailing over the rooftops of London.

"COME DOWN!" shouted the porter.

Tom leaped on to the banister, and slid down. The boy felt his bottom become hotter and hotter as he slid down faster and faster. Very soon he realised he couldn't stop.

"Arrrggghh!" he cried.

"What's the matter, young Mr Thomas, sir?" called up the porter.

"MY BOTTOM IS ON FIRE!"

"That's all we need now," remarked Robin.

The boy slid
down the banister
faster and faster. The
friction was so great
that the old pyjamas the
porter had found for him
started smoking at the seat.
"ARRRGGGHHH!"
screamed Tom.

"MY BOTTOM REALLY IS ON FIRE!"

"Yes, dear, we heard you the first time," replied Robin unhelpfully.

"George, grab that fire extinguisher!" shouted the porter.

The boy did as he was told, but in lifting it up by the handle he must have set the cylinder off, as foam started spraying all over everyone.

SPLURGE!

"Watch where you are pointing that thing!" screamed Amber, as she now resembled a giant Mr Whippy ice cream.

"I can't turn it off!" cried George.

As Robin, too, was covered head to foot, he remarked, "I haven't the faintest idea what's going on any more."

"HELP!" screamed Tom. "SOMEBODY CATCH ME!"

With the fire extinguisher still spraying foam everywhere, the porter was also soon covered.

SPLURGE!

Desperately, the porter tried to rub the foam out of his eyes to get into position to catch Tom.

"I CAN'T SEE ANYTHING!"

cried the porter.

"Join the club," remarked Robin.

Looking over his shoulder, Tom could see that he was heading straight for Amber.

"AMBER! TRY AND CATCH ME!" he shouted.

"MY ARMS ARE BROKEN!"

she called back.

WHIZZ!

Tom shot off the end of the banister.

WHOOSH!

He flew through the air.

WHIZZ!

And landed on top of Amber.

SPLAT!

Sending her wheelchair speeding off backwards…

RATTLE!

They hit the wall with a tremendous…

WALLOP!

...and landed in a crumpled, foamy heap on the floor.

CRUNCH!

Then the splurging finally stopped.

"Great news, everybody!" announced George.

"What?" said the others.

"I've worked out 'ow to turn this thing off!"

"Just in time!" said Robin sarcastically.

"I am glad my arms and legs are already broken," said Amber. "Otherwise they *would* be broken."

Tom examined the seat of his pyjamas. It was black and charred.

"Well, come on!" said the porter.

"What?" replied the Midnight Gang.

"We have to catch a flying old lady!"

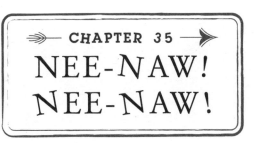

CHAPTER 35

NEE-NAW!
NEE-NAW!

The Midnight Gang rushed over to an ambulance. The old rusty vehicle rattled as its engine was still running.

"Pile in, everybody!" barked the porter.

Everyone worked together to lift Amber and her wheelchair into the back of the ambulance.

"Right, who wants to be lookout?" asked the porter.

"I am not sure I'm the best candidate," mused Robin, indicating the bandages over his eyes.

"I'll do it!" said Tom. It sounded fun.

"Excellent, Mr Thomas, sir, I'll just strap you to the roof!" he replied.

"You'll what me to the what?!" demanded Tom.

"There's no time to argue! Nelly is flying high over London as we speak!"

The man whipped off his old leather belt, and with some difficulty hoisted himself up on to the roof of the ambulance. He strapped the belt to the siren and gave it a tug to make sure it was secure.

"Right! Up you get!" said the porter as he offered his hand to hoist Tom up.

Tom stood on the roof of the ambulance and held on tight to the belt.

"You are my eyes!" said the porter, sliding down the windscreen. "You tell me when you spot the old girl!"

"OK!" said Tom.

"Ready?" said the porter.

"Y-y-yes!" replied the boy.

The ambulance sped off.

BRMMM!

As the vehicle zoomed off into the night, Tom's eyes searched the black sky. *What fun Sally's missing*, he thought. Suddenly these imaginary adventures had taken a whole new turn. Far off in the distance, Tom was sure he could just make out the large cloud of balloons with an old lady dangling beneath it pass in front of the full moon.

"There she is!" cried Tom.

"Which way?" asked the man.

"Straight ahead!"

BRMMM!

The ambulance sped up.

Tom had to hold on tight as the porter drove the ambulance as fast as it could possibly go. Which was surprisingly fast.

"LEFT! LEFT! DEAD AHEAD!" shouted the boy.

The ambulance skidded round corners, went the wrong way down one-way streets and even mounted the pavement in pursuit of the flying old lady.

"I don't see why we have to be in such an awful rush," muttered Robin, sitting up front between the porter and George. "What goes up must come down. I am sure the old dear will land somewhere, and she can find her own way back to the hospital."

"I don't care so much about the ol' lady," remarked George. "I just want me balloons back! It's my go next."

"I can't believe how uncaring you two boys are!" said Amber, who could hear everything from the back. "That poor old lady desperately needs our help. And what's much more important is that we are having a ride in an ambulance! Faster, man! FASTER! And put the sirens on!"

The porter smiled and did what he was told.

NEE-NAW!
NEE-NAW!
NEE-NAW!

Up on the roof, the noise was deafening. Tom now had to shout instructions at the top of his voice for the porter to have any chance of hearing him.

"RIGHT!"

Far up in the sky, the old lady was skimming the roofs of some of London's most famous landmarks: St Paul's Cathedral, Nelson's Column in Trafalgar Square and the Houses of Parliament. Then the hem of Nelly's nightdress caught on the tallest spire of Westminster Abbey.

The nightdress was whipped clean off in an instant.

"Oooh-hoo-hoo!" laughed Nelly. "I AM IN THE NUDDIE!"

Indeed she was.

"SHE'S NAKED!" shouted Tom. Now he was staring at some wrinkly balloons and a wrinkly bottom.

"OH NO!" the porter shouted up. "IT ACTUALLY LOOKS LIKE SHE IS HAVING THE TIME OF HER LIFE!" shouted down Tom.

Then DISASTER struck.

The branches of a tall tree wiped out half of Nelly's balloons. Immediately the naked old lady began descending at an alarming rate.

Nee-naw! Nee-naw!

"STOP! SHE'S RIGHT ABOVE US!" shouted Tom down to the porter.

The man slammed on the brakes and the ambulance came to an abrupt halt.

The lady came straight down on the roof with a...

BUMP!

...knocking out Tom in the process.

THUD!

CHAPTER 36

THE UNWELCOMING COMMITTEE

It was now a tight squeeze in the back of the ambulance. Tom was lying on the stretcher, out cold after being knocked out for the second time in two days. Amber was in the middle in her wheelchair. On another stretcher was Nelly, wrapped in a blanket to cover her modesty. The old lady was sitting up, buzzing from her first balloon flight.

"When am I going flying again?" she asked brightly.

"You're not!" replied George curtly.

The boy was grumpy that his dream of flight had been so cruelly snatched from him by this old dear.

"It was me who was

meant to be flyin' tonight. You're not even a member of the Midnight Gang!"

"The Midnight Gang? That sounds jolly exciting! Please may I join?"

"NO!" snapped George. "After tonight, you will never ever ever be a member of the Midnight Gang!"

"You could have put another 'ever' in that sentence for emphasis," mused Robin.

"EVER! EVER! EVER! EVER!" said George.

"Mmm, still not quite enough 'ever's," muttered Robin.

"Oh shut up! Porter?"

"Yes, Mr George, sir?"

"I don't suppose we 'ave time to stop off at an Indian takeaway? I need to get a couple of dishes for me newsagent mate."

"I hate to disappoint you, sir, but we are in rather a hurry," replied the porter.

"I thought not. It's just that 'e is starvin' hungry…"

"I am sorry, sir."

"Not even a poppadom?"

"It's not wise to stop, sir."

"I'll tell ya now, my mate Raj is not goin' to be 'appy."

George had insisted that all the remaining balloons be taken back to the hospital for another attempt. Reluctantly, the porter had tied them to the lights on the roof and they were bouncing up and down on the ambulance as they sped through the streets of London.

The man drove the vehicle as fast as he could. They had to get back to the hospital as quickly as possible. Everyone had to be in their beds before Dilly had found a way out of the gift shop, and also of course before Matron woke up.

Otherwise they would all be in deep, deep trouble.

Tom was beginning to come round on his stretcher. The boy was muttering to himself.

"I was on the cricket pitch. The ball. It flew towards me. Hit me on the head. I blacked out…"

"No, dear," corrected Robin. "That was last time. This time you were hit by a naked old lady."

"What?" demanded Tom, suddenly alert.

"Smashing to see you again!" said Nelly cheerfully.

The porter looked at his watch, and put his foot hard down on the gas.

BRMMM!

Having the sirens on meant he could speed past any traffic that was on the road.

NEE-NAW! NEE-NAW! NEE-NAW!

A broad smile spread across his face. The porter was clearly loving playing at being an ambulance driver for the night, quite a step up from his usual job of pushing patients around the hospital on trolleys.

Finally, he swung the ambulance round the last corner, and the entrance to **LORD FUNT HOSPITAL** came into view.

As the porter drove towards the building, he noticed there were a number of people waiting outside. They were all staring towards the approaching ambulance. As he drove closer still, he realised this was not a welcoming committee.

More an unwelcoming committee.

The immaculately dressed hospital principal, Sir Quentin Strillers, was standing on the steps. On one side of him was Matron, and on the other was Dilly the cleaning lady. All had furious looks on their faces. Next to them was a pair of burly and unsmiling nurses.

The Midnight Gang had been well and truly

BUSTED!

CHAPTER 37

NOT A LAUGHING MATTER

The Midnight Gang was marched to the principal's office. It was a huge oak-panelled room with a giant oil painting of Lord Funt, the founder of the hospital, over the mantelpiece. The porter and the four children were gathered together in the middle of the room.

Sir Quentin Strillers sat behind his desk as if he was a king on a throne. The principal was the most important person at **LORD FUNT HOSPITAL** and he certainly looked the part. The man sported an immaculate pinstripe suit, with a natty pink tie and a matching handkerchief flowing from his breast pocket. A gold watch on a chain hung from his waistcoat.

Standing over his shoulder, like a bird of prey sitting on its perch, was Matron. It was now 5am and dawn was just breaking. The sun was shining right into the children's eyes. All except Robin were squinting furiously.

Sir Quentin began by listing the gang's crimes in his rich, fruity voice. He delighted in every vowel and syllable.

"Drugging a staff member with special chocolates. Stealing a large quantity of balloons. Imprisoning the cleaning lady in the gift shop. Sending the hospital's most elderly patient into the air. Smashing a skylight. Hijacking an ambulance. Reckless driving."

"Is that all?" joked Robin.

The other children and the porter couldn't help but chuckle at his comment.

"THIS IS NOT A LAUGHING MATTER!" bellowed the principal. "And, no, that is not all. That is just tonight! Do you care to explain yourselves?"

"It was all my fault!" said Tom. "I am the ringleader."

All the other members of the Midnight Gang turned to the boy. What was he doing? Tom was getting himself into even more trouble than he was already in, and he was already in a lot of trouble.

Sir Quentin pursed his lips. "Really? But you have only been in the hospital for two nights."

"It was me!" said Robin. "I am the ringleader."

Matron scoffed. "I hardly think so. You can't see a thing."

"It was me!" announced Amber. "I am the ringleader!"

"Really, young lady?" asked the principal.

"She can't have done it all on her own, Sir Quentin," hissed Matron. "Not with those broken arms and legs."

"Maybe not," replied the principal. "What about you, boy?"

"It wasn't me," replied George. "I 'ad nothin' to do with it. As if I would want to fly through the air with the aid of stolen balloons!"

The other three children were not impressed with George at all.

"It was me, sir," announced the porter, who had been quiet up to this point.

"*What* was you?" asked the principal, his eyes narrowing.

"It was my fault these children went on all these night-time adventures. I filled their young minds with crazy ideas. Please don't punish them in any way. I am solely to blame, sir."

The children turned to the porter, stunned into silence. Could they let him take all the blame? That hardly seemed fair, as their friend had only helped their dreams come true.

CHAPTER 38
DEEP, DEEP TROUBLE

"Matron?" said the hospital principal, as he sat passing judgement in his office.

"Yes, Sir Quentin?" she replied.

"Take this awful gang of children back to your ward. Put them all in their beds and make sure they stay there. I don't want one of these children to leave your sight. Do you understand me, Matron?"

"Yes, Sir Quentin, sir," said Matron. She smiled at the children, smug that she had won.

The children all shuffled out of the room.

Robin couldn't resist a parting shot at Sir Quentin. "By the way, I love what you've done to your office. The décor is a delight!"

"Thank you!" said the man, before remembering that the boy had bandages over his eyes and was being sarcastic.

"OUT!" ordered the principal, shooing them towards the door. "I have to deal with the porter now."

As they passed through the doorway, Tom, George and Amber turned back to look at their friend. There was terrible sadness in his eyes, but the porter just managed a smile.

"Goodbye, young sirs and madam," he muttered.

It sounded like a final goodbye.

Matron slammed the door behind them.

Then the sound of the principal shouting echoed down the corridor.

Tom's heart ached for the porter, being bawled at like that.

As what was left of the Midnight Gang traipsed towards the lift, Matron turned on them with glee.

"Right, you lying, deceitful little creatures!" she began. "You are in deep, deep trouble!"

PING!

Once they were inside the lift, Tom couldn't stop himself from asking, "Matron, what is going to happen to him?"

"Don't you worry. None of you will ever see that dreadful man again. And as for your revolting gang…"

All the children turned to her.

"…that is well and truly over."

The lift doors closed.

PING!

Needless to say, the mood in the children's ward in the morning was sombre. Sally was eager to know what had happened, but no one was keen to tell her. The night had been such a disaster.

Even a visit from the ever-sunny Tootsie couldn't lighten the atmosphere.

"Toast or cornflake?" said the lady as she pushed her food trolley between the rows of beds. "Toast or cornflake?"

"Cornflakes, please," said Tom.

"Right you are, Thomas!" replied Tootsie.

She then proceeded to pick up the cereal box and pour the contents into a bowl. True to her word, there was just the one cornflake. It fell into the bowl with a pathetic little…

CL*I*NK!

"Is that it?!" asked Tom.

"I did say 'cornflake' not 'cornflakes'. Sorry, but I only had one left. I saved it for you as I know you like them."

"Don't eat it all at once!" called Robin from across the ward.

"Would you like some cold tea poured on top?" Tootsie reached for the tea urn. The boy shuddered at the memory of yesterday's soggy mush of a breakfast.

"No, thank you, Tootsie! Milk, please."

"I don't have any milk today either, but I do have half a sachet of ketchup?"

"I am starving. I suppose I could give it a try!" replied Tom gamely.

"Very good!"

The lady squeezed a tiny amount of the red sauce on to the cornflake.

"There you go!" she said, handing over the breakfast that would have left an amoeba hungry.

"Please may I have a piece of toast too?" asked the boy hopefully. After last night's adventures, he was mightily hungry, and that one cornflake was not going to be enough.

Tootsie opened a metal door on her trolley where the hot food was stored. "Oh no. The boss of this place, Strillers, has made us make so many cutbacks at the hospital, you see? I'm all out of toast. Sorry."

Then she moved on to George, cheerfully calling out, "Nothing! Absolutely nothing for breakfast!"

Unsurprisingly there weren't any takers.

"Oh dear!" said Tootsie. "I don't know what the matter is with all you children this morning."

"The matter is…" interrupted Matron. She was standing right behind Tootsie. Again, it was as if she had appeared from nowhere. "...these disgusting children are in a great deal of trouble. They have broken every rule in the hospital."

"But they all seem like such nice children," replied the dinner lady.

"Don't be fooled! They are nothing more than common thieves and liars."

All the children dropped their heads in shame.

"Except Sally," said Matron.

Tootsie looked over to the little girl's bed. "She is still asleep. Dear little thing."

"And because of these four nasty little children here, the porter has been sacked."

"No!" Tootsie couldn't believe it. "Sacked?"

"Yes! On the spot this morning. He deserved it. Despicable man. I always knew he was up to no good. Sir Quentin Strillers demanded he leave **LORD FUNT HOSPITAL** immediately."

"Oh no. Oh no no no. Oh no no no no no.

The porter didn't deserve that. He is such a sweet and kind man. And he has been at the hospital forever. For as long as anyone can remember!"

"Of course he deserved it. Helping these children with their stupid little night-time games!" thundered Matron.

"But **LORD FUNT**'s was his life!" protested Tootsie.

"The poor man had nothing else. No wife. No children.

No family to speak of. Legend has it that the day he was born his mother abandoned him on the steps of this hospital."

"Who can blame her?" laughed Matron. "What mother could bear to look at a child so ugly?"

It was the saddest story Tom had ever heard. Sometimes Tom felt as if he had been abandoned by his parents by being dumped at his boarding school, but nothing compared to this.

Tootsie shook her head. "Poor, poor man," she muttered. "I must see if he is all right. He might need a sofa to sleep on, or someone to cook him a hot meal."

"That foul being does not deserve your sympathy! Or anybody's! Filling these children's heads with ridiculous ideas. I always said he is as ugly on the inside as he is on the outside."

"That's not true!" protested Tom.

"The porter *is* beautiful on the inside!" said Amber. "He is the kindest person I know!"

"I doubt you even know what kindness is, Matron!" said Robin.

"Yeah!" joined in George. "You ol' moo!"

For a moment it looked as if a revolution was about to begin.

"SHUT UP!" snapped Matron.

The children were scared into silence.

"What vile little creatures you all are, sticking up for that... MONSTER! I don't want to hear another word out of any of you all day!"

Only Tootsie was bold enough to break the silence. "Matron?" she asked.

"WHAT?!"

"Do you have any idea how I can get in touch with the porter?"

"Not a clue! Looking at the state of his clothes, and smelling him, I wouldn't be surprised if he was homeless, and lived in a cardboard box somewhere. Ha! Ha!"

"Well, wherever he is, I will say a little prayer for him tonight," said Tootsie.

"He'll need more than prayers to help him now!" scoffed Matron. "His pathetic little life is finished. He will never get another job after being sacked from here! Now, Tootsie, finish up the breakfast as quickly as you can and get out of my ward."

"Yes, Matron!"

"I need to think of the best way to punish these wicked, wicked children."

With that, the lady spun on her heel and stalked back to her office.

CHAPTER 40
CHOCOLATE FOR BREAKFAST

Standing with her food trolley in the children's ward, Tootsie watched Matron go. Then she looked over to Tom.

"Have you finished your cornflake?" she asked.

Unsurprisingly the boy had. "Yes, thank you."

"How was it?"

"I'll be honest, not great."

"Sorry."

"*Tootsie!*" hissed Amber.

"Yes, child?"

"Please try and find the porter," began the girl. "I can't believe how awful the story of his life is. I feel so guilty. He was only trying to help us and now he has been given the sack. I need you to tell him that we all love him very much, and miss him terribly. And tell him Amber is really, really sorry about what has happened."

"And Robin is sorry too!" said Robin.

"And George!" said George.

"And please tell him no one is more sorry than me, Tom," said Tom.

"Well, hang on a second, please – I am the most sorry," protested Amber.

"It was my dream that went wrong! So really I must be the most sorry," added George.

"Oh, please let's not get into an argument over who is the most sorry!" interrupted Robin. Then with a smile he added, "Obviously it's me!"

"If I find him, I'll tell him you are all really, really, really sorry!" announced Tootsie.

"Good plan!" said Tom.

"What are we going to have for breakfast?" asked Amber.

"Have you got any more chocolates, George?" asked Robin.

"Yes," he replied. "I've got a secret stash 'idden away somewhere. It's my last tin, but let's share 'em out."

The boy opened up his pillowcase to produce a tin.

He threw a handful over to everyone else's beds.

"Thanks, George," said Tom.

"Well, the Midnight Gang was great while it lasted," said Robin. "I got to conduct an orchestra of medical instruments. Amber got to go to the North Pole. George here got to levitate off the ground for a few seconds…"

"Oh yes! That was a dream come true!" said George sarcastically.

"But, Tom, you never had your chance. I am curious; what would you have wished for?"

"I have been thinking about this all morning," replied Tom.

"Yes?" asked Amber.

"Well, when you made me swear the oath to the Midnight Gang, there was the part about putting your friends first."

"'That I will always put the needs of my brothers and sisters in the gang over my own'?" said Amber.

"That's it!" replied Tom.

"So?"

"So that's exactly what I want to do. Someone else's needs on this ward are much greater than mine. And I wanted to give my wish to somebody else."

"Who?" asked Robin.

"Sally!" replied Tom.

"Of course!" replied Robin.

CHAPTER 41

ONE LAST ADVENTURE?

"Sally wants to be in the Midnight Gang more than any of us," said Tom. "Yet time and time again she was told she couldn't be."

"We didn't want to make Sally more ill," said Amber. "The adventures were often dangerous. We were only thinking about her."

From the corner of the children's ward, Sally spoke up. "But surely in life we should all have at least one dream come true."

"We all thought you were asleep!" said Tom.

"I was and I wasn't," replied the little girl. "The treatment I had yesterday really wiped me out. But I am feeling much better today."

"That's good," said Amber.

"Thank you so much for giving me your wish, Tom. That's the best present I could ever have."

"That's all right, Sally," replied Tom. "I am just sorry you will never get to use it."

"Why?" asked Sally.

"Because the Midnight Gang is no more," replied Amber.

"The grown-ups 'ave closed us down," added George.

"Just because we made a ninety-nine-year-old lady fly over the rooftops of London!" said Robin. "Naked. It's outrageous!"

"Ha ha!" Sally laughed. After a moment, it looked like the laughter was causing her some pain. One by one the children got out of their beds, and formed a circle round Sally.

"Are you all right?" asked Tom, holding the little girl's hand.

"Yes, yes, I am fine," replied Sally, clearly lying. "And you are sure the Midnight Gang can't have one last adventure?"

The children shook their heads sorrowfully.

"But what would have been your dream?" asked Tom.

"Yes," said Amber. "We'd all love to know."

Sally looked up at them. "You are going to think I am stupid, but…"

"We are not going to think you are stupid," replied Tom. "Whatever you say."

"I wanted to go to the North Pole, even though my arms and legs are broken!" said Amber.

"I wanted to conduct an orchestra, even though I couldn't see them," added Robin.

"And I wanted to fly!" laughed George. "And I am twice as 'eavy as any one of you!"

Sally smiled.

"Well…" The little girl was growing in confidence now. "I want to live a big, beautiful life!"

"What do you mean?" asked Tom.

"I've spent so much of my life in hospital and missed so much already. Sometimes I think I'll never get out of this place. I may never have my first kiss. Get married. Have children."

All the others had tears welling in their eyes.

"Don't feel sad for me," said Sally. "But please, please, please can the Midnight Gang have one last adventure – the adventure of a lifetime?"

"WHAT ARE YOU WICKED CHILDREN ALL DOING OUT OF YOUR BEDS?" bellowed Matron.

She had appeared from nowhere, as she had a habit of doing. "I have been far too soft on you all. This children's ward is going to be run very differently from now on. Back to your beds THIS INSTANT!"

The children did as they were told and retreated to their beds, the boys helping Amber into hers first.

"Now! No one is to leave their beds unless I say so. Do you understand?"

There were reluctant mutters of, "Yes, Matron."

"I said,

'DO YOU UNDERSTAND?'"

The children answered louder this time. "Yes, Matron."
"GOOD!"

Just as Tom was sliding back into his bed, Matron called out to him, "Not you, boy."

Tom wondered what he had done.

"All your test results came in this morning," announced Matron.

"Yes?" the boy gulped. He knew what was coming.

"Yes. Surprise, surprise! It turns out there is absolutely nothing wrong with you. You were faking it all along, you deceitful little snake."

"But—" protested Tom.

"SHUT UP!"

bellowed Matron. "You are to leave the hospital at once. Your headmaster is here to collect you right now!"

CHAPTER 42
THE ESCAPE

Tom had all but forgotten about St Willet's. Even though the boy had only been at the hospital for a couple of days, the place already seemed like his home, and the other children his family.

"Charper!" called out the headmaster from across the ward. At his posh boarding school, the teachers never used your first name.

"Yes, sir?" replied Tom. It was as if he was already back at school.

"Time to leave, boy." The headmaster was a portly gentleman with long sideburns and little round glasses. The man always wore a heavy tweed suit, a cardigan and a bow tie. A waft of pipe smoke followed him everywhere he went. It was as if the headmaster had travelled through time from at least a hundred years ago to the present day. The school prided itself on not having changed in hundreds of years, so the old-fashioned headmaster, Mr Thews, suited it perfectly.

Matron stood next to him at the end of the ward. "Chop chop!" he ordered.

"What about my mum and dad, sir?" asked Tom.

"What about them, boy?" replied Thews.

"I thought they might be coming to pick me up?"

"Oh no no no, they are miles away!" scoffed the headmaster.

Tom looked downcast.

"It was only a little cricket ball on the head, boy!" continued Thews. "It might have knocked some sense into you! Let's not forget the St Willet's school motto – '*Nec quererer, si etiam in tormentis*'. Translate that from the Latin, boy!"

"'Never complain, even if you are in great pain.'"

"Excellent!"

The motto was written underneath the school's coat of arms, and emblazoned on every blazer.

As the other children in the ward

looked on with sadness, Tom pulled the curtain round his bed to get changed back into his cricket whites. The boy took as long as he could. He didn't want to leave his friends.

"For goodness' sake, get a move on, boy!" ordered Mr Thews. "Stop dilly-dallying."

Tom pulled the grass-stained cricket jumper over his head and stepped out from behind the curtain.

"Have you heard from my mum and dad at all?" asked Tom hopefully.

The headmaster shook his head, and smirked.

"Not a whisper! They never call. They never write. It's almost as if they have forgotten all about you."

Tom bowed his head.

"Come on, Charper, what are you waiting for?" demanded the headmaster.

"I just need to say goodbye to my new friends."

"There isn't time for that, boy! Come on! Quick smart. You have a great deal of schoolwork to catch up on since you have been in here."

"You heard what your headmaster said, child!" snapped Matron. "Get a move on!"

As Tom made his way along the shiny floor of the ward, he glanced either side to take one last look at his new friends.

Sally, Amber, George and Robin all lifted their hands in a silent wave.

The Escape

"The matron has told me all about your appalling behaviour since you have been here at the hospital," announced Mr Thews.

Tom said nothing.

"A 'gang' indeed? Getting out of your beds in the middle of the night? You have soiled the good name of St Willet's school."

"Sorry, sir."

"Sorry isn't good enough, boy!" snapped the headmaster. "You will be punished severely as soon as we are back at school."

"Thank you, sir."

"Goodbye, boy," said Matron. "I hope I never see your nasty little face again."

Tom turned his head and took one last look at his friends. Sally smiled back, but Thews yanked Tom's arm and the tall doors swung open and shut. The headmaster frogmarched Tom along the corridor, his hand placed firmly on his shoulder. Tom felt like an escaped prisoner who had been captured and was being returned to prison.

He had to do something.

Anything.

Sally deserved her dream to come true more than any of the children, and time was running out.

The lifts were ahead. Tom knew if he was going to escape he had to think fast. Within moments, he would be in the headmaster's car making the long journey back to his boarding school in the country.

Up along the corridor, Tom spotted the replacement porter with a large trolley of laundry. The man was standing by a hatch in the wall, stuffing bags of laundry into a chute. Tom knew the chute led all the way down to the basement of the hospital. A child could fit in there, but not a grown-up.

The new porter moved off and Tom realised this was his only chance.

The boy wrestled himself out of his headmaster's grasp and ran off ahead.

"COME BACK HERE, BOY!"

bellowed Thews.

"Goodbye, sir!" said Tom as he took a running leap headfirst down the chute.

CHAPTER 43

A WALL
OF BLACK

"AAAAAAAA
AHHHHH!" cried
the boy as he slid at speed down
the laundry chute. Tom had
leaped in on the top floor, and it
was an awfully long way down to
the bottom. Forty-four floors, in
fact. It was pitch black, and as he
slid he realised he was gathering
speed at an alarming rate.

At the bottom of the chute
a small square of light became
visible in the darkness.

This became bigger and bigger until Tom realised he was travelling through it and falling through the air.

"NOOOO!"

he cried.

T
H
U
D!

The boy landed in the huge basket of laundry bags in the basement. He breathed a sigh of relief to still be alive. Then with some difficulty Tom scrambled out of the basket and disappeared off into the darkness of the basement.

Right now he desperately needed somewhere to hide.

His headmaster might still be on the top floor, but very soon half the hospital would be looking for him.

Tom dashed past the laundry room.

𝕋𝕠𝕠 𝕟𝕠𝕚𝕤𝕪.

Then he passed the freezer room.

Too cold.

Then he passed the storeroom.

Too spooky.

Tom stopped dead still for a moment. In the distance, the boy could hear the sound of footsteps. The sound was becoming louder **and louder.** Whoever was down there with him was moving closer and closer. It sounded like an army.

Light from torches bounced off the walls.

Tom could make out the shadows of dozens of nurses coming towards him.

In desperation, Tom tried to open a door.

Locked.

And another.

Locked.

And another.

Locked.

As the shadows grew closer, a wave of panic washed over the boy.

"Thomas?" It was Matron, who was leading her army of nurses through the basement. "We know you must be down here!"

"That nasty little boy is in a great deal of trouble," said the headmaster, who Tom could just make out in the darkness running alongside Matron. "CHARPER? CHARPER?"

Shadows bounced off the walls of the basement at all angles, making it seem as if this army was coming at Tom from all sides.

Tom tried turning the handle of one last door.

CLICK!

It opened.

Inside it was pitch black, and Tom felt scared. He took a deep breath and stepped in, closing the door behind him.

A wall of black.

All the boy could hear now was his own breathing.

Yet he sensed that he wasn't alone.

"Hello?" Tom whispered. "Is anybody there?"

In the shadows, the boy saw a pair of eyes staring back at him.

"AAARRRGGGHHH!"

screamed the boy.

CHAPTER 44

HOME

"Shush!" came a voice out of the gloom.

A match was struck and the unmistakable outline of the porter's face was lit up by a burst of light. Tom breathed a sigh of relief at seeing it was his friend.

The porter lit a candle and the room flickered into view.

"What are you doing down here?" demanded the boy.

"This is where I live," slurred the man. "It's my home."

"But I thought you were sacked!"

"I was. But I had nowhere else to go. Now what are YOU doing down here?"

"I'm hiding," replied the boy.

"Who from?"

"My headmaster. Matron. An army of nurses. Everyone really. My headmaster came to take me back to my boarding school. But I didn't want to go."

"Well, you can't stay down here forever," said the porter.

"No," replied the boy. He had run away without a plan and was beginning to realise he was in even deeper trouble for fleeing than he had been before. "So this is really your home?"

"Yes, Mr Thomas, sir," replied the porter. "Look!" The man moved the candle around the room so the boy could see. "I have everything I need right here."

The porter indicated a filthy-looking mattress lying on the floor in the corner. "My bed. There is the cooker."

There was a tiny gas stove with a stack of tinned food next to it.

"Wardrobe."

The porter pointed to a large cardboard box that had some crumpled clothes hanging in it.

"But why haven't you got a proper home?" asked the boy.

The man sighed deeply. "This hospital is my home. I've been here since I was a baby. Back then, the doctors tried operation after operation on me."

"What for?"

"To try and make me look 'presentable'. But none of them worked. I was a patient here for years and years. Then when I was getting too old for the children's ward a job came up at the hospital and I took it. Just a simple job. Moving things and people around. I was sixteen then and I have been here ever since."

"But if you had a job then why didn't you find a place to live?"

"I tried. The council helped me find a tiny one-bedroom flat in a block not far from here. But the problem is that sometimes folk think you are frightening because you look frightening. I couldn't get any peace there. Locals would paint horrible words on my front door. Put nasty letters through my postbox telling me to go. They said I was frightening the children. I was shouted at. Spat on. Had a vicious dog set on me. One night

when I was asleep a brick smashed through my window. So I came back here and hid. Nobody ever knew I was living down here. This is my home."

Tom's eyes glistened with tears. He felt sad but guilty too. Just like so many other people, Tom had thought the worst of the porter just for the way he looked. The boy stared around the porter's damp, dank room. It wasn't much, but it was a home. It was more than Tom had. With his parents living abroad and him being bundled off to a boarding school, the boy never had anywhere he could call home.

"It's not the Ritz hotel, I know, but at least it was convenient for work!" The man chuckled to himself. "But, now I have lost my job, I don't know where to go."

"If I had a home, I'd invite you to stay."

"That's very kind of you."

"But I am sad to say that I don't."

"They say 'home is where the heart is'. Where is your heart, Tom?"

The boy thought for a moment, before replying, "I suppose with the children on the ward. And with Sally the most."

"Poor little lamb."

"She never got to have her dream come true."

"No. What about your mum and dad?"

"What about them?"

"Is your heart not with them?"

"No," replied the boy quickly. "They don't care about me."

"I am sure they both love you very much."

"I am sure they don't. They never call. They never write. I hardly ever see them."

"I am sure they are thinking about you."

Tom said nothing.

"Look at the two of us!" remarked the porter. "A couple of lost souls, aren't we?"

"I am so sorry that you lost your job here at the hospital," said Tom. "All of us on the children's ward were sorry. In fact, we had an argument over who was most sorry."

"Did you, now? Well, don't you worry yourselves about little old me. I knew what a risk I was taking helping the Midnight Gang. It was worth getting sacked for."

"Are you sure?"

"Yes! I'd do it all again. Just to see the smiles on all you children's faces over the years."

"But can't we just try and beg Strillers to give you your—?"

Before the boy could say another word, the porter whispered, **"Shush!"**

The man pointed to the door.

Tom listened. There were footsteps outside, and the sound of metal doors being rattled.

"It must be the search party! They have found me! Is there another way out?"

"No!"

"Oh no!"

"We'll have to hide!"

"Where?"

"You conceal yourself in the cupboard, and I'll hide under the bed."

Tom climbed into the cardboard box, while the porter pulled the mattress over himself.

"The candle!" hissed Tom.

The porter blew it out just as the large metal door swung open.

$CL_{U_{N_{K!}}}$

The torchlights shone inside, moving slowly around the room.

Home

Tom didn't dare breathe as Matron and the headmaster stepped inside, an army of angry-looking nurses behind them.

"Come out, come out, wherever you are…" hissed Matron.

CHAPTER 45
A
ONE-WINGED
PIGEON

"Something or someone's in here. I know it," whispered Matron as her torch threw light on the darkest corners of the room in the hospital basement.

"It looks like a load of old junk to me," replied Mr Thews. "Let's move on."

"No," Matron replied. "That smell." The woman sniffed the stale air. "It's strangely familiar."

As he crouched in the porter's cardboard wardrobe, Tom had the strangest sensation. It felt as if his little finger was being nibbled. When he looked down, he saw that indeed it was. His little finger was being nibbled by a pigeon.

Without thinking, the boy shook his hand to get

the creature off him. This sent the poor pigeon skimming across the floor.

"*SQUAWK!*"

squawked the bird.

"Aaarrrggghhh!" screamed Matron.

"It's just a pigeon!" said Mr Thews.

"I hate the dirty beasts. They are like rats with wings! Nearly as bad as children."

"Now can we please move on?" asked the headmaster.

"Yes," she replied. "I must inform the maintenance department to shoot that blasted creature at once. I would love to come down myself with a bucket and drown it, but sadly I just don't have time."

"That is a shame," mused the headmaster. "That would have been a pleasure."

"I am so pleased you feel the same way as me, Mr Thews. I do love a touch of cruelty."

"There is nothing more enjoyable. I like to be cruel to my pupils at St Willet's. That keeps them under my complete control. Any letters sent from family members, I burn before they reach the boys. Tom's parents wrote every week, but I put their letters straight on the fire! Ha! Ha!"

Tom couldn't believe what he was hearing.

"Ooh! That must give you so much pleasure."

"It does, Matron, it does. There is nothing better than the feeling of absolute power!"

"Tom's stupid parents have been calling the hospital. Desperate for news of their son. But I put the phone straight down on them!"

"Ha! Ha! That nasty little insect deserves everything he gets. I can't wait until I get my hands on him. The punishment will be severe!"

"Make him eat cold cabbage every meal for a year?"

"Mmm. The food at St Willet's is worse than that."

"Make him wash in bog water?"

"The boys have to do that already."

"Make him do a cross-country run in his pants?"

"Mmm. When it's snowing!"

"What a wonderfully wicked idea, Mr Thews!"

"Thank you, Matron. There's no time to lose. We must find that boy now!"

"Let's split up. You check the deep freezer, Mr Thews. Some of the children were in there the other night."

"Right away, Matron."

"And I will check the boiler room. Do shout if you find the little worm."

"Oh, I will!"

The pair turned round, and with the nurses in tow rushed off to continue their search.

When the sound of all their footsteps was distant, the porter emerged from under the mattress.

"What an evil pair!" said Tom, his heart racing.

"They are as bad as each other," replied the porter. Then he lit his candle, and the basement room flickered back into view. To Tom's surprise, the man rushed over and scooped up the stunned bird in his hands.

"Why did you have to do that to Professor Pigeon?" he whispered.

"'Professor Pigeon'?" asked Tom, a note of disbelief in his voice.

"Yes! It's because she's so very clever. She's my pet pigeon. And, look, she only has one wing."

Tom looked down. Indeed, the bird had a stump where one of her wings should have been.

"How did she lose it?" asked the boy.

"She was born that way. Her mother turfed her out of the nest just after she had hatched."

"That's cruel."

"That's what animals do. She was the runt of the litter, I suppose. Just like me."

Tom listened as the man stroked his pet pigeon, which *cooed* in pleasure.

"What do you mean?"

"Well, I was only a few hours old when my mum left me on the steps of this hospital."

"I am so sorry."

"She left me here in the middle of the night, so no one saw her face."

"So you have no idea who your mother is?"

"Or was? No. But I forgive her. And I miss her too, though I never knew her."

"Why did she leave you here?"

"I suppose Mum hoped I would be looked after better here at the hospital. Maybe she thought the doctors and nurses could help me? And do something about this."

The porter pointed to his misshapen face and tried to smile through the pain.

"I am so sorry," said the boy.

"Don't be sorry, young Mr Thomas, sir. I still love my mother. Whoever and wherever she may be. No one wanted to adopt me, so Lord Funt, who founded this hospital, let me stay in the children's ward. Funt was a kind man. Not like this new fellow."

"Amber told me the Midnight Gang began on the ward long ago, and has been passed down through all the patients."

"That's right."

"But no one knew which child started the gang. Do you know?"

"Yes, I do," replied the porter. The old man smiled to himself.

"Who was it then?" the boy asked, his eyes widening with excitement.

"It was me," replied the porter. "I was the child who started the Midnight Gang."

CHAPTER 46
PRINCE CHARMING

"You?!" asked Tom. The boy's head was spinning at the news.

"Yes, Mr Thomas, sir. Me!" slurred the porter.

The pair was sitting in the man's dark, damp home, down in the basement of **LORD FUNT HOSPITAL**.

Tom smiled. "Now it all makes sense! Why you helped us!"

"Well, I have been helping the children in the ward live out their dreams for fifty-odd years."

"So why did you start the Midnight Gang?"

"Same reason as you children today. I was bored. I think Lord Funt might have suspected us kids were up to something. But I know above all else he wanted his patients to be happy. Funt turned a blind eye to our midnight adventures."

"So what was your dream?"

"Well, sometimes the other children in the ward would be cruel to me. They'd call me names: Monster Man, Elephant Boy, the Creature."

"That must have hurt."

"It did. But children only bully when they themselves are unhappy. They were just taking out their unhappiness on me. Just like Matron and your headmaster, I suppose. I was made painfully aware of how I looked, and I dreamed of being a handsome prince, and rescuing a beautiful princess."

"So did you?" asked the boy.

"Yes. In a way. I was only about ten years old. Me and the other children in the ward made a pantomime horse out of blankets and a broom. Two of the children hid under it, one was the front of the horse and the

other was the back. I rode in on the horse to save the princess who was imprisoned in a tower. At the top of the stairwell, in fact."

"Who was the princess?"

"She was called Rosie. One of the patients. Eleven years old. The most beautiful girl I had ever seen in my life."

"What was she being treated for?"

"She had a weak heart. The night that Rosie played my princess was the most magical night of my life. When I rescued her, she gave me my first and last kiss."

"Whatever happened to Rosie?"

The porter hesitated for a moment. "Soon after that night her heart stopped beating. The doctors and nurses did everything they could to save her. But she didn't make it."

The porter bowed his head. Even though he was talking about something that happened more than fifty years ago, he felt the pain of it like it was yesterday.

"I am sorry," said Tom. He reached out his hand and rested it on the man's shoulder.

"Thank you, Mr Thomas, sir. Rosie was kind to me. She didn't care that I looked like this. She could see past it. Her heart may have been weak, but it was big. Losing Rosie made me realise something."

"What's that?"

"That life is precious. Every moment is precious. We should be kind to each other. While there is still time."

CHAPTER 47

NOTHING IS IMPOSSIBLE

The pair sat in silence in the basement room for a moment, before the porter broke it.

"Now, Mr Thomas, sir, you are going to get in big trouble if you stay down here a moment longer."

The man gave some crusts of bread to Professor Pigeon. The bird picked them up and hopped over to her nest, where Tom saw there was a number of tiny pigeon eggs.

"You are going to have babies!" said the boy.

"Well, they aren't *my* babies!" laughed the man. "But, yes, Professor Pigeon is about to become a mother herself. I am so looking forward to them hatching."

The porter studied the boy for a moment before remarking, "That bump on your head has gone down completely."

"It still hurts," lied Tom.

"I'm not stupid. I know you fooled that poor Doctor Luppers so you could stay in the hospital longer."

"But—!"

"You might fool him, but you can't fool me! Now come on, let's get you upstairs to find your headmaster. You need to go back to your school right away."

"No!" replied Tom defiantly.

The porter was taken aback by this. "What do you mean 'no'?"

"I mean 'no', not until the Midnight Gang can get back together for one last mission."

The porter shook his head wearily. "There is no way, Mr Thomas, sir. The whole hospital is on to you kids now. There can be no more missions for the Midnight Gang."

Tom wasn't giving up. "But you said yourself that life was precious! Every moment is precious!"

"I know but…"

"Then we have to make Sally's dream come true. Let's be kind, while there is still time."

"But not tonight, Mr Thomas, sir. It's impossible!" replied the porter.

"**Nothing is impossible!** There has to be a way," said the boy. With a sense of drama, he stood up and marched over to the door. "**If you won't help us, then that's fine! We'll do it ourselves!**"

Tom opened the door. Just as he was about to walk out, the porter stopped him.

"Wait!" he said.

With his back to the man, Tom smiled to himself. He knew he had hooked him; now he just had to reel him in. The boy turned round to face the porter.

"Just out of interest," began the man, "what is young Miss Sally's dream?"

Tom hesitated for a moment. He knew what he was about to say was far beyond anything the Midnight Gang had ever attempted before. "Sally wants to live a *big, beautiful life*... in just one night."

CHAPTER 48
AN AWFULLY BIG ADVENTURE

"Let me get this straight, Mr Thomas, sir," slurred the porter. "Young Miss Sally wants to live a lifetime, seventy, eighty years perhaps, over just one night?"

"Exactly! She desperately wants to experience everything life has to offer!" said Tom with a gulp. The boy knew this was going to be the hardest dream of all for the Midnight Gang to pull off.

"Everything?"

"Everything. Listen, I know it sounds crazy, but—"

"It sounds beautiful," interrupted the porter. The man stroked his one-winged pigeon one last time before setting it down gently on the ground. "We'll need a plan," he said.

"I've already got one!" replied the boy.

"What?"

"We put together a little show. Make Sally the star."

"What will the show be about?"

"It will be snapshots, little scenes of what happens in life. First kiss…"

"First job?"

"Having a baby, even!"

"That's a brilliant idea!" exclaimed the porter.

Tom could feel his cheeks glowing red with embarrassment. He had never been told he had thought of anything brilliant before.

"Thank you," replied the boy.

"This is a big dream. Bigger than big. Gigantic! We'll need props and costumes and all sorts."

"Yes! There is so much stuff to find. Me and the other children will need to get straight on to it."

"And we'll need to make a list of what all those special moments for Sally might be."

"Yes."

"What an incredible final mission for the Midnight Gang! Come on, Professor Pigeon," said the porter, scooping up the bird in his hand and placing it in his pocket. "We are going to have an awfully big adventure."

CHAPTER 49

TWO LEFT FEET

Now that Tom was officially "on the run", not only from the hospital but also his school, it was going to be very difficult for him to get back up to the children's ward from the basement. Forty-four floors and hundreds of patients and doctors and nurses separated the boy from his destination.

"If I am spotted, it's all over," he said.

"I know," replied the porter. "We'll need to disguise you."

Tom spied a rusty old hospital trolley in the corner of the porter's den.

"Could I pretend to be a very ill patient?" he asked. "You could cover me with a sheet and then push me back up to the children's ward. No one will know it's me."

"An excellent plan, young Mr Thomas, sir..." said the porter.

Tom was just about to dive on to the trolley when the man said, "But you are forgetting something. Something big."

"What's that?"

"Sir Quentin Strillers fired me on the spot for what going forward we shall call 'the-flying-old-lady incident'. So we are both going to need a disguise."

"Sorry, I forgot," replied the boy, downcast. "Maybe it would work better if we reversed the roles?"

"What do you mean?"

"I mean, I can be the doctor and you be the patient! We could cover you in a sheet."

"I have one right here!" replied the porter.

The man picked up a white sheet so old it had gone grey. He shook it out and clouds of dust filled the basement room. The blizzard of dust made the pair cough and splutter.

"Sorry!" said the porter. "But, Mr Thomas, sir, how

is anyone going to believe that you are a grown-up?"

The boy was unusually short for his age.

"There must be something we can do. I just need to be taller. If only we had some stilts!"

"I have the next best thing!"

The porter scrabbled around in a corner of his den. He discarded all sorts of items that must have been thrown out by the hospital. Rubber gloves, stethoscopes, sample jars, metal dishes, tongs... all flew past Tom until the porter finally found what he was looking for.

A pair of prosthetic legs. These were made of plastic and meant for people who had lost a leg through an accident or illness.

"This pair of legs should work a treat!" said the porter as he passed them to the boy.

Except they weren't really a pair.

Tom examined them.

"There are two left feet," said the boy.

"Who is going to check?!" replied the porter confidently.

"You can borrow a pair of my trousers to cover the legs."

"OK, let's try it!" replied Tom.

After a few moments, the pair checked the coast

was clear and emerged from the porter's room in the basement of the hospital. The porter had lent Tom his cleanest pair of trousers, which were of course still covered in a thick layer of grime. He had also found two left shoes to slip the prosthetic feet into. The shoes weren't matching, of course. One was a black brogue, and the other a white plimsoll.

Tom had put on a long white coat, and to complete the look the porter had drawn a moustache on the boy with soot. Unsteady on his new legs, Tom wobbled out along the corridor, pushing the old rusty trolley. Underneath the dusty sheet on the trolley lay the porter, rather enjoying being pushed for a change.

"To the children's ward! And quick!" ordered the man.

"I'll go as fast as my legs can carry me!" replied the boy.

"Deeper voice, please!"

"What?"

"If people are to believe you are a grown-up, you

are going to have to talk in a **deeper voice."**

Tom tried again, this time in a much **deeper voice. "I'll go as fast as my legs can carry me."**

"Too

deep

now!"

The boy sighed and tried again.

"I'll go as fast as my legs can carry me."

"Perfect!" said the porter.

Tom set off, immediately tripped over and sent the trolley careering into a wall. The porter banged his head on it. Hard.

"Ow!"

"Sorry!" said Tom.

"At least now I have a real injury!" said the porter.

The pair chuckled, and set off as quickly as they could for the lifts.

CHAPTER 50
POPPADOMS

"There's no way Matron is going to fall for the snoozy-pellets-in-the-chocolates trick again," said Tom as the pair travelled up in the lift.

"I know," slurred the porter, lying on the trolley. "That's why we are going to make an unscheduled stop."

The man reached out his hand from underneath the sheet and pressed **36**.

"What's on that floor?" asked Tom.

"That's the pharmacy."

PING!

The doors opened on to the thirty-sixth floor.

On his "stilts", Tom felt like a gazelle taking its first steps. He struggled to keep upright, and held on to the trolley for dear life. It was late and the corridor was empty of people. Under the sheet, the porter called out instructions to the boy.

"Turn left…"

CRASH!

"Mind the bench."

BANG!

"And the counter!"

BOOM!

"Best to slow down when going through the doors!"

"Sorry!" said Tom. The boy couldn't help it. Balancing on these prosthetic legs was going to take a great deal of getting used to.

"Now, when we reach the pharmacy, you need to ask for a syringe and fifty millilitres of sleep serum."

"What are we going to do with it?"

"That will put Matron to sleep until morning."

"But up close they are never going to believe I am a doctor!" protested Tom.

"Don't worry. The old gentleman who works nights at the pharmacy is deaf as a post and blind as a bat."

"Let's hope so!" replied Tom.

"Now we need to get a move on! It's just up ahead on the left."

At that moment, a patient in his pyjamas with all his fingers bandaged up trundled round the corner and the trolley bashed right into his belly.

"OW!" screamed Raj.

"I am so sorry!" replied Tom, in something of a panic.

"Deeper!" whispered the porter from under the sheet.

"Who said that?" demanded Raj.

"Oh, just my patient under here!" replied Tom in a deeper voice. **"He is saying the pain in his bottom... is 'deeper' than it was."**

"Mmm. Well, Doctor…"

"Who is the doctor?" asked Tom.

"You are," replied Raj, looking very puzzled.

"Oh yes, sorry. I forgot."

Raj stared at this strange person for a moment. Tom started to feel sweat run down his face.

"Well, Doctor, I was looking for the children's ward. A young customer, one of my top hundred favourites, actually, from my newsagent's shop, is a patient here."

"George!" exclaimed Tom.

"That's his name! He took my takeaway order last night and I still haven't got my food. It was a very small order. Just poppadoms, onion bhaji, samosa, chicken jalfrezi, aloo chaat, tandoori king prawn masala, vegetable balti, peshwari naan, chapati, aloo gobi, matar paneer, tarka dhal, poppadoms…"

"You said poppadoms already…"

"Yes, I know, Doctor. I want two portions. One is never enough. Mango chutney, paneer masala, pilau rice, bharta, lamb rogan josh."

"Is that everything?"

"Yes. I think so. Did I say poppadoms?"

"Yes. Twice!"

"I need three portions of poppadoms. You can never have enough poppadoms."

"Clearly not!"

"So can you direct me to the children's ward?"

"Don't let him go up there!" whispered the porter from under the sheet.

"Up where?" demanded Raj.

"His bottom!" replied Tom. "It is very painful."

The newsagent looked utterly bemused. "Now please, Doctor, tell me where it is. I have been up and down this hospital for hours looking for the place."

"Lie!" whispered the porter.

"Lie? What does he mean 'lie'?" said Raj.

"He means he wants to lie down. Take the weight off his bottom."

The newsagent stared at the figure under the trolley. "He is lying down."

"Y-y-yes," spluttered Tom. "He is now. He was very slightly sitting up before. Like maybe one degree."

"For the last time!" exclaimed Raj. "Where is the children's ward?"

"Go down in the lift to floor three."

"Yes?"

"Walk across the corridor to the far side of the hospital."

"Yes?"

"You'll find a set of stairs."

"Yes?"

"Go up one flight."

"Yes?"

"Come out of the double doors."

"Yes?"

"Take your first left."

"Yes?"

"Second right."

"Yes?"

"Go to the end of the corridor. You'll see a set of double doors ahead of you."

"Yes?"

"Ignore those."

"Yes?"

"First left."

"Yes?"

"Are you getting all of this?"

"No. None of it."

Tom pointed randomly down the corridor. "That way."

"Thank you!" said Raj. "I will be sure to save you a small piece of poppadom."

"That is very kind!" replied the boy as he watched the poor man disappear off down the corridor.

"Good work, Doctor!" joked the porter. "That's the last we'll ever see of him! Now, to the pharmacy!"

CHAPTER 51
SUSPICION

Tom steered the trolley along the corridor. At the end of it was a hatch in the wall where the pharmacist handed out medicines.

An elderly man was sitting on the other side of the sliding glass window. Mr Cod wore a hearing aid and thick, round glasses. He was busy sipping noisily from an impossibly large mug of tea.

Tom took a deep breath, and addressed him. "Good evening…"

"Deeper!" came another whisper from under the sheet.

The boy tried again, deeper this time. **"Good evening."**

Mr Cod didn't look up.

"He's not responding!" whispered the boy.

"Cod must have forgotten to turn his hearing aid on again," said the porter. "You are going to have to shout!"

"GOOD EVENING!"

shouted the boy.

"THERE'S NO NEED TO SHOUT, DOCTOR! I'M NOT DEAF!" shouted

Mr Cod.

"Sorry!" said the boy.

"What did you say?" asked the elderly man, holding a cupped hand to his ear.

"Maybe you need to turn your hearing aid on, Mr Cod!"

"I can't hear a word you are saying! Let me turn my hearing aid up."

Mr Cod put his mug of tea down and fiddled with the dial on his hearing aid. When nothing appeared to happen, he banged the box with his

knuckles and the gadget whistled into life.

"Right, what can I do for you, Doctor?" Mr Cod asked.

Tom smiled. The plan was working.

"I need a syringe and fifty litres of sleep serum, please."

A look of shock crossed Mr Cod's face. "What do you need all that for? Are you going to put a hippopotamus to sleep?"

"Millilitres!" came a whisper from under the sheet.

"Who said that?" demanded Cod.

"It was my patient," replied the boy.

"How come your patient knows more about what he needs than you? You are supposed to be the doctor!"

The boy thought for a moment. "Well, my patient is a bit, to use the correct medical term, 'bonkers'. The poor man thinks he's a doctor. He's delusional!"

"That still doesn't explain why he knew the correct dose," replied the elderly man.

Cod had a point.

"Well," began Tom with trepidation, "he is so delusional, he is actually a brilliant doctor. In fact, I am taking him down to the operating theatre right now."

"Why?"

"To perform an operation. That's why we need all that sleep serum."

Mr Cod shook his head wearily. "I thought I had seen it all. Fifty millilitres of sleep serum coming right up."

The chemist hopped off his stool, and scuttled off to the back of his pharmacy.

"Well done," said the porter.

"Shouldn't that be, 'Well done, Doctor'?" chuckled the boy.

"Don't get cocky, young sir!"

When Mr Cod returned with the serum, he stumbled slightly and dropped the medication on the counter. As he bent to pick it up, he peered down at Tom's feet.

"You have two left feet!" observed Mr Cod.

"Yes," replied the boy. "Most people only have the one left foot, but I am lucky enough to have two."

"I have never heard of such a thing!" exclaimed the chemist.

"Well, apart from not being the best at ballroom dancing, it's never held me back. Thank you so much."

Mr Cod peered through his thick glasses, looking at this "doctor" with deep suspicion.

"You just need to sign for it here," muttered Cod. He pushed a medical form across the counter.

"Thank you," replied the boy. "Have you got a pen?"

The chemist shook his head. "Another doctor who doesn't have a pen!"

Cod produced a biro from the top pocket of his lab coat. "Now, don't think you can make off with it!"

The chemist rolled the pen across the counter and it fell to the floor. The boy leaned down to pick it up, and lost his balance.

"Arrrgghh!"
THUD!

Tom was sprawled out on the floor. His prosthetic legs had become detached.

Cod peered down.

"Your legs have fallen off!" he said.

"Yes. I won't need them any more," replied the boy. "Do feel free to give them to anyone who might want them."

"You aren't a doctor!" exclaimed Cod. "You are a child! You must be the boy everyone in the hospital is looking for!"

"He is a doctor!" said the porter from under the sheet. "Just like me!"

"You are both up to no good!" shouted Cod. "I am calling the hospital security!"

The boy grabbed hold of the trolley and sped off down the corridor, crashing through the swing doors with a terrific

BANG!

"We'd better get a move on!" said the porter. "Have you got the syringe?"

"Yes," replied Tom. "What are we going to do with it?"

"Simple! Stick it in Matron's bum!"

CHAPTER 52

A PAIN IN THE BUM

*PIN*G*!*

The lift doors opened on to the forty-fourth floor. Just along the corridor were the huge swing doors to the children's ward.

"How are we going to stick this into Matron's bum?" asked the boy. He was holding the syringe full of the sleeping serum as he wheeled the trolley along as quietly as possible. "She is going to be watching everything like a hawk."

"We must use surprise, young Mr Thomas, sir!" replied the porter. The man poked his head out from under the dirty sheet on the trolley. "Matron cannot see us coming. Or we are **BUSTED**."

"We have the trolley. That could give us some

speed," said Tom, thinking out loud.

"Yes. Of course, in an ideal world we need Matron facing away from us, bending over."

Tom brought the trolley to a stop. They were now just a few paces away from the doors.

"I've got an idea!" said the boy excitedly. "Have you still got Professor Pigeon in your pocket?"

"Yes, of course," replied the porter. "She's coming on the adventure with me."

"Good! Then we can let her loose in the children's ward. The bird is bound to scuttle all around and Matron is sure to be distracted. You heard her say how she hated pigeons!"

"It's brilliant, sir. Quite brilliant."

The pair went down on to their hands and knees and crawled across the corridor that led on to the children's ward. Tom pushed one of the tall swing doors open a little, and held it ajar. Looking out of the window to the glow of Big Ben's clock face, he saw it was now just minutes to midnight.

The boy peeped through the gap between the doors. All the lights in the ward were off, and the children were sleeping in their beds. Tom could see the silhouettes of George, Amber and Robin. However, he couldn't make out Sally's bed as it was in the far corner of the ward. Some light spilled from Matron's office, where she sat bolt upright, her eyes

scanning the ward for any signs of movement.

The porter reached into his pocket, and brought out his uni-winged pet. Tom then pushed the door slightly more ajar, so the bird could scuttle through. However, Professor Pigeon did not want to move. Perhaps the bird did not want to be separated from her master? Whatever the reason, the creature was determined to

stay put. So the porter picked up his pet and set her down just inside the ward. But, instead of scuttling off, the faithful bird just lingered by the doors pecking at the floor.

"Go, Professor Pigeon! Go! Fly like the wind!" urged the man.

Again, the bird did nothing. This was clearly not an animal that was going to win a TV talent competition any time soon. That was a shame, as what with having only one wing Professor Pigeon had a great backstory.

"Shoo! Shoo!" encouraged the porter. But still the bird did absolutely nothing.

So the porter had no choice but to squeeze through the gap in the doors on his hands and knees. From there he ushered his bird further into the room towards Matron's office at the end.

Out of the silence came a booming voice.

"WHO GOES THERE?"

It was Matron. She had seen the porter. The plan was unravelling faster than a falling ball of string.

Tom had to think fast.

Through the gap in the doors, he could see the lady rushing out of her office. So he pushed the trolley back down the corridor. Then he ran alongside it and jumped on, syringe in hand.

BANG!

The trolley smashed through the swing doors.

Ahead, Tom could see the perfectly round bottom of Matron. She was bent over, trying to pull the porter up from the floor.

"It's you, Porter! Now get up, you revolting man! I want you out of my ward this instant! Do you hear me? THIS INSTANT!"

From behind her behind, her head appeared. She must have heard the whir of the wheels on the trolley.

WHIRRR!

"Thomas?" she cried.

But it was too late!

The needle of the syringe stabbed into her bottom.

"OUCH!" she cried in pain.

As Tom pushed the top of the syringe, the sleeping serum surged in.

Matron's body arched up.

Then...

THUD!

The lady was immediately fast asleep on the floor, snoring loudly.

"ZZZZ-ZZzz ZZzz-ZZZZ..."

CHAPTER 53
BONG!

Amber, George and Robin were out of their beds now, and peering down at their enemy sprawled out on the floor. The normally immaculate matron looked decidedly undignified. Her arms and legs were splayed like a starfish, and a pool of drool was leaking from her mouth.

"OK, Midnight Gang, it's time to go to work!" said Tom. "Where's Sally? Sally?"

Amber fell silent as Tom looked over to Sally's bed.

It was empty.

Tom looked to the other children for an explanation. Their sad faces told a story.

"What?" asked the boy. "Where's Sally?"

"While you went missing, Tom," began Amber, "poor Sally took a turn for the worse."

"Oh no," said Tom. In all the excitement about the plan, he had forgotten how ill the little girl was.

"So she was taken down to the isolation ward," added Robin.

"But what about her dream?" pleaded Tom.

The children all shook their heads.

"Not tonight, Tom," replied Amber. "We can't."

"Sorry, Tom," said George, resting a hand on his friend's shoulder.

"At least we tried," muttered the porter. "But I am afraid it's all over."

There was silence in the children's ward.

BONG!

Big Ben began to chime midnight.

BONG!

The gang all listened...

BONG!

...and bowed their heads.

BONG!

Time was running out.

BONG!

Fast.

BONG!

This moment was slipping away from them.

BONG!

They had to do something!

BONG!

For Sally!

BONG!

The little girl deserved to have her dream come true...

BONG!

... more than any of them.

BONG!

There had to be a way!

BONG!

Just as the final chime ended, Tom announced, "You are wrong."

CHAPTER 54

TOGETHER

"Here we go…" muttered Robin.

"Pray continue!" said Amber, a sarcastic tone in her voice. She was a girl who was not used to being told she was wrong about anything ever.

"If Sally has been taken to the isolation ward, that is all the more reason why we have to do it tonight," said Tom. "I promised her something once, and I let her down. I can't let her down again."

"But if she's in the isolation ward, Tom, she must be too ill!" exclaimed Amber.

"Let Sally decide whether she is up to it or not," replied Tom. "Look, we all know we are going to get better. Robin, you will see again. Amber, your arms and legs will heal. George's operation has been a success, though you do need to cut down on the chocolates."

"I know!" replied George. "From now on I'll cut down to just one tin a day."

Tom smiled, even though George wasn't joking.

"Sally doesn't know when she will get better. She told us herself. The fact that she's been sent down to the isolation ward scares me. It must mean she's got worse. We need to make Sally's dream come true tonight!"

"The boy's right," agreed the porter.

"Yes, yes, yes," said Amber, speaking for the two boys, "but her dream, to experience the whole of life, it's just so…"

"Big?" suggested George.

"Yes!" replied Amber. "The Midnight Gang has done some cool things. We've all had fun…"

"I never got to fly," moaned George.

"Oh, there's always somebody who's not happy," muttered Robin.

"…but this is so much more than that," continued the girl.

"That's why we need to try. For Sally's sake," said Tom. "Give her the big, beautiful life she deserves. Come on! Please! We can do this together. As a gang. I know we can. Let's vote. Who's in? Raise your hand!"

The porter and the two boys put their hands up. They all looked to Amber.

"Amber?" said Tom. "Are you in?"

"Yes of course I am in!" shouted the girl. "I just can't raise my hands, can I?"

"OK, Midnight Gang," said Tom. "Let's go out with a *BANG!*"

CHAPTER 55
NESTLED IN THE PILLOWS

Tom told the other children his vision for how he thought they could make Sally's dream come true. Everyone in the Midnight Gang, including its founder member, the porter, added ideas of their own.

Next, the porter took Amber, George and Robin down to the operating theatre to start preparing everything. Meanwhile, Tom headed alone to the isolation ward to collect Sally. His heart was pounding with the thrill of it all. However, nothing could prepare him for what he was about to see.

After ducking down to pass the nurse's station, the boy pressed his face up against the glass that looked on to Sally's room. A mess of wires and tubes snaked around her bed. The room was cluttered with silver machines bleeping and computer screens blinking. These were monitoring her heartbeat and blood pressure and breathing. In the middle of there somewhere was a little girl. Sally's bald head was nestled deep in pillows, her eyes closed.

Tom hesitated. He felt it was wrong to disturb her. Perhaps he should go and find the others and tell them Sally's dream couldn't come true after all?

Just as Tom was about to turn to go, the girl's eyes opened. A flicker of a smile crossed her mouth as she recognised the friendly face. With a slight nod of her head, she beckoned the boy into her room.

So as not to alert the nurse at her station down the corridor, Tom opened the door as slowly and silently as he could. He stepped inside and tentatively approached the bed.

Sally looked right at him and asked, "What took you so long?"

Tom smiled.

The game was on!

CHAPTER 56
NONE SHALL SLEEP

The operating theatre was a huge, gleaming room, with a wide glass window on one side. Big bright lights were attached to the ceiling. They were so bright that you couldn't look directly at them or you would see stars.

Tom wheeled Sally on her bed into the centre of the room.

"I am so excited!" said Sally.

"Good. We are just about to begin. Is everyone ready?" asked Tom.

"Ready!" replied Amber, Robin and the porter.

"Not quite ready!" called out George, who was fiddling with something. "Right, now I am ready."

"Have you selected the music, Robin?" asked Tom.

"Yes!" Robin replied. "As soon as you hear it start, let's all begin."

As Robin placed one of his CDs into his player, the others took their respective places in the operating theatre.

The music started. It was the unmistakable sound of the world's most famous opera aria, *"Nessun Dorma"* by Puccini from the opera *Turandot*.

The English translation for *"Nessun Dorma"* is "None Shall Sleep", a fitting motto for the Midnight Gang. The recording was sung in Italian and the translation is:

None shall sleep!
None shall sleep!
Even you, O Princess,
In your cold room,
Watch the stars,
That tremble with love and hope.

The words could have been written about Sally. It was a fittingly majestic piece of music to accompany the next few minutes, which would represent a lifetime.

From her bed, Sally watched with wonder as the children worked around her in the operating theatre. Robin was standing at the back of the room with a slide projector. As he heard his beloved opera aria begin, he flicked a switch on the projector and the machine whirred into life. The first slide was projected on to the wall of the operating theatre right in front of Sally. It read: **EXAM RESULTS.**

Sally giggled. "Oh no!"

Then Tom placed a square black hat on Sally's head that had been made from a cereal box. Next he handed her a rolled-up piece of paper in a red bow. Sally unrolled the "exam certificate" to see to her delight that she had received A*s in every subject imaginable.

"Yes!" she said. "I always knew I was a genius! It's just no one else knows it yet!"

Then Robin pressed the button for the next slide:
FIRST CAR.

The porter gave Tom a dinner plate to pass to Sally. It had been drawn on with a black felt-tip pen to make it look like a steering wheel. The words "Aston Martin", the famous luxury-car manufacturer, had been written on it. Then the pair started spinning Sally's bed around as the girl pretended to drive. To add to the sense of speed, George ran in the opposite direction past Sally's bed holding small fake, plastic Christmas trees.

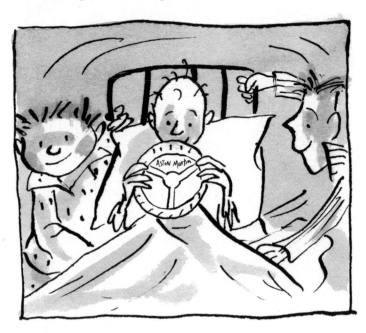

Then came: **FIRST KISS.**

The porter then handed Tom a bunch of flowers and pushed him towards Sally. The boy bristled at the thought, so he passed on the flowers to George. George obviously wasn't a fan of kissing either, as he passed the flowers on to Amber. Amber took charge, and ordered Tom to wheel her towards Sally. Then she handed her friend the flowers and gave her a peck on the cheek.

As this chapter of Sally's life ended, another began:

A HOLIDAY IN THE SUN.

The porter produced two dining trays that George and Tom strapped to Sally's feet with string. Then the porter handed the girl a piece of rope with a handle at the end. At first Sally looked completely mystified about what was happening. The other end of the rope was attached to Amber's wheelchair. Then the porter pushed the wheelchair forward, which pulled Sally upright on to the trays.

She was water-skiing!

Sally laughed at the cleverness of it all.

Next was: **WEDDING DAY.**

As Sally sat back down on her bed, Tom placed a
bridal veil on her head. The veil had been made out of
boxes and boxes of white tissues. George handed Sally
back the bunch of flowers and instantly the girl looked
like a bride on her wedding day.

Next the porter produced a black top hat that was really a bucket. This was for the groom. But who was going to marry Sally tonight?

The porter put the hat on Tom's head, who put it on George's head, who put it on Robin's head, who had no one's head to put it on.

"What is going on?" asked Robin.

"You are gettin' married," said George.

"To a girl?" asked the boy.

"Yes!"

"That's never going to happen!" replied Robin. He took off his hat and passed it back to George, who put it on Amber's head.

"It looks like you are marrying Amber," said the porter.

"I would love to!" replied Sally.

The porter then handed Amber a large metal ring, which she placed on Sally's finger. Despite it not being gold and too big and clearly from a shower curtain, a tear rolled down Sally's cheek. The wedding might not have been real, but the feeling was. Tom and George had bags of rice that they threw over the happy couple. The porter flicked the lights on and off to mimic a camera's flash. It was the perfect wedding shot.

"Tell me what you can see!" called out Robin eagerly.

"Sally is crying," replied Tom.

"Happy tears or sad tears?"

"Happy!" cried Sally, wiping them away.

Robin smiled and pressed the button for the next chapter: **BABY.**

At seeing this word, Sally began to giggle. How were they going to conjure up a baby? Surely they hadn't "borrowed" one from the maternity ward?! George put on a nurse's hat and handed the girl a bundle wrapped up in a blanket. Sally felt the bundle move and opened it out to reveal Professor Pigeon under there. The bird was wearing a little baby's bonnet fashioned from a rubber surgical glove.

On seeing the bird's face she smiled, and she stroked its head tenderly. It cooed.

Then the Midnight Gang was straight on to the next chapter in Sally's life: **JOB.**

The porter directed the boys to slide into view a hospital screen that was painted to make it look like the door to 10 Downing Street, the famous home of the British Prime Minister. They placed it behind Sally, who chuckled.

"I always knew I'd get the top job!"

Meanwhile, the porter placed a crown on Amber's head. This was made from a strip of cereal-packet cardboard. Brightly wrapped sweets had been sticky-taped to the side. The different-coloured shiny papers in white, green and red (Matron had eaten all the purple ones) gave the appearance of diamonds, emeralds and rubies. Robin flicked the light switch on and off.

CLICK!

It was like the flash of a camera, taking a photograph of the Prime Minister meeting the Queen.

GRANDCHILDREN read the next slide.

"So soon!" cried Sally as she was handed six little baby pigeons that must have just hatched, wrapped up in a towel. Professor Pigeon had become a mother, and Sally a grandmother!

"Six babies!" cried Sally.

"Sextuplets!" said Amber.

"Not real babies, I hope!" called out Robin.

"Baby pigeons!" replied Sally. "I love them all!"

As "*Nessun Dorma*" reached its thrilling crescendo, the Midnight Gang circled their friend's bed with the props and costumes from her life. Amber put her crown back on. George pushed the door to 10 Downing Street round and round. The porter took the six baby pigeons back and pulled the rope so the girl could water-ski again.

"*Nessun Dorma*" came to a magnificent end, with the opera singer holding the last note for what seemed like forever. Sally was helped to stand up and took a bow.

"This is my life!" cried the girl.

The whole group cheered her.

"HOORAY!"

At that moment out of the corner of his eye, Tom spotted something. On the other side of the huge window in the operating theatre a crowd had gathered. The hospital principal, Sir Quentin Strillers, was standing at the front, and behind him were a dozen or so serious-looking doctors and nurses staring at them.

None Shall Sleep

The porter noticed that Tom was distracted by something.

"What's the matter, Tom?" he whispered.

"Look!" replied the boy.

The porter, Amber, George and Sally all followed the boy's gaze to see the group standing on the other side of the glass.

"Oh no," said Tom. "We are in deep, deep trouble."

CHAPTER 57
MAKE HER SMILE

There was an eerie silence for a moment while the two groups stared at each other through the glass that divided the operating theatre from the observation room.

Then the most unexpected thing happened.

The hospital principal, Sir Quentin Strillers, began to applaud. The doctors and nurses behind him began clapping too. From the looks on their faces, it was clear they were deeply moved by what they had seen.

"What is going on?" asked Robin.

"It doesn't look like we are in trouble after all," replied Tom.

Strillers rushed into the room, flanked by his doctors and nurses.

"That was beautiful!" the man cried. "Breathtakingly beautiful."

"Thank you!" said Amber. "It was mainly my idea."

Tom looked over to George and the porter, and rolled his eyes.

"Well then, young lady, mighty congratulations are in order. Do you know what the most moving part was?"

"Me pressing the buttons on the projector?" asked Robin.

The principal didn't get the boy's dry sense of humour so answered him seriously. "No, young man, although your button-pressing was top notch. What was truly wonderful was to see this little patient of mine smiling."

With that, he patted Sally on the head awkwardly. The girl had been smiling right up to that moment. Now Sally was rather annoyed that this man she barely knew was patting her like a dog.

"All the doctors and nurses, in fact everyone here at **LORD FUNT HOSPITAL**, have been working so hard to help young Susie..."

"Sally," said Sally.

"Are you sure?" asked Strillers.

"Yes," replied Sally. "My name is Sally. Definitely. I'd remember that."

"She can change her name to Susie if that helps you, Sir Quentin," offered up Robin.

"No, that won't be necessary, boy," said the principal, once again not getting the joke. "But one thing we never did, never even thought of doing, was to make her smile."

"Thank you so much, Sir Quentin," said Amber, taking all the credit again. "My name is Amber, by the way, if you are thinking of recommending anyone for a damehood."

"Sir Quentin, it's very important you know we couldn't have done it without this man," said Tom, hugging the porter tightly. "He is the man you sacked!"

"Yes, yes," murmured Strillers. "Well, my decision had been troubling me all day. After all, it was the great Lord Funt himself who took this man in as a baby."

The porter smiled.

"He grew up here," continued Sir Quentin. "And he has had a job here for many years."

"Forty-four years!" remarked the porter.

"Is it really? Well, it's safe to say that **LORD FUNT HOSPITAL** is your home. It always has been. And always will be. Seeing the look of joy on Sally's face has made me realise you might just be the best person we have here at the hospital. Forgive me, gentlemen and ladies, but this man is worth a hundred doctors and nurses."

The doctors and nurses murmured their disapproval.

"Thank you, Sir Quentin, sir," replied the porter proudly.

"We look after the children's illnesses and injuries well here at the hospital," continued Strillers, "but we don't do nearly enough for their happiness. Porter-man, sorry, what is your actual name?"

"I don't know," said the porter. "I was never given one."

"What? Why?" The principal was flabbergasted. "Surely everyone has a name!"

"My mother gave me up the day I was born," continued the porter. "And nobody adopted me. So I suppose no one ever thought to give me a name."

"That isn't right!" said Robin, being serious for once.

"We must find you a name," said Sir Quentin. "Is there one you fancy?"

"I like 'Thomas'!" replied the porter.

Tom smiled bashfully.

"Thomas it is!" announced the principal. "And of course, Thomas, you have a job here for life. Just promise me there will be no more flying-naked-old-lady incidents…"

Thomas Senior smiled. "I'll try."

"Now, it's very late," said Sir Quentin, checking the gold pocket watch that hung from his waistcoat on a chain. "I need you to all go back to your beds at once."

"Yes, sir," murmured the children.

"Let me put a call up to Matron to collect you from down here," said the principal.

"Oh no!" jumped in Tom a little too fast, remembering that she was sprawled out like a starfish on the floor. "Our friend here, Thomas Senior, can take us up."

"Off you go then. And I don't want to hear another peep out of you all night!"

Thomas Senior smiled, and began to wheel Sally's

bed out of the operating theatre, as the other four children followed.

"No. Sally needs to go back to the isolation ward," ordered Sir Quentin.

The children all looked downcast.

"But I don't want to," protested Sally. "I want to be with my friends. Please."

The principal looked distinctly uncomfortable. Surrounded by his doctors and nurses, he needed to be seen to do the right thing. This girl was ill; the hospital had a duty of care. The man looked around at everyone.

Murmurs of "let her be with her friends", "make the girl happy" and "give her what she wants" could be heard.

"**All right!**" bellowed the principal. "Sally, you may go back to the children's ward. But just for tonight."

 came a shout.

Everyone in the room celebrated the good news.

"But I want lights out straight away, and you all need to get a good night's sleep."

"As if we would dream of doing anything else, sir," replied Robin with a smirk.

CHAPTER 58
TONIGHT IS FOREVER

It was three in the morning by the time the Midnight Gang were all back in the ward.

Even though she had always been vile to them, the children felt guilty about Matron lying in a heap on the floor. So, with Thomas Senior's help, they placed her on one of the beds so she would have a good night's sleep. They even tucked her in. Thomas Senior took himself off to Matron's office to have a doze.

As Matron snored away…

"ZZZZ, ZZzz, ZZzz, ZZZZ, ZZZZ"

…the Midnight Gang played games, shared sweets and told stories. When the excitement had died down

a little, and George, Robin and Amber began to doze off, Sally turned to Tom.

"Thank you, Tom," she said. "It was so kind of you to give me your dream."

"That's what the Midnight Gang is all about," replied the boy. "Putting your friends first."

"Well then, you have been the best friend ever."

"Thank you. You should try and get some sleep."

"I just wanted to ask you…"

"Yes?"

"What would your dream have been? The one you wanted to come true."

"I know it sounds stupid, especially next to yours, but…"

"What?"

"I just want to see my mum and dad."

"That's not stupid."

"I miss them so much."

"Where are they?"

"Far away. In the desert somewhere. When I was hiding in the basement, I overheard Matron say she had put the phone down on them again and again."

"What?"

"And my headmaster burned their letters."

"That's disgusting!"

"I know. I used to think they didn't care about me…"

"Now, you know they do."

"I hope so, Sally. I just want to see them."

"You will. I know it," said Sally with a twinkle in her eye. After a moment, she added, "I have to say it's been the most amazing night, Tom. It's been the adventure of a lifetime."

"Good. You deserve it. You are very special. But you need to go to sleep now."

"I don't want to. I want tonight to last forever."

But it couldn't.

Nothing can.

As much as all the children on the ward wanted time to stand still and for them all to live in this moment forever, the morning sun shone through the high windows.

The night was over.

CHAPTER 59
"MY BOTTOM HURTS!"

As dawn broke, all was finally still and quiet on the children's ward. But just as Tom closed his eyes to finally try to get some sleep he heard a familiar voice echoing down the ward.

It was Sir Quentin Strillers.

"**Matron!**" he bellowed. "**What are you doing lying in bed?**"

Tom opened one eye.

"Wake up, woman!" shouted Strillers. "I don't pay you to sleep on the job!"

The matron stirred. "Where am I?"

"You're in bed!"

"At home?"

"No, in the hospital!"

"Am I ill?" she asked. The sleeping serum that Tom injected into her must have really knocked her out. "My bottom hurts!"

"No, you are not ill, Matron! But you are in deep, deep trouble!"

The other children all began waking up. They could barely contain their glee at hearing their adversary being told off like this.

"I am so, so sorry, sir," she said.

"Sorry isn't good enough, Matron! I am taking you off the children's ward at once. You are now on toilet-cleaning duty until further notice."

"Yes, sir. Sorry, sir,"
replied Matron. The lady
stumbled out of bed,
and scrambled out of
the ward, one shoe on,
one shoe off, clutching
her sore bottom.

Seeing that Sir Quentin
was approaching Tom's bed, the boy shut his eyes in
a pantomime of sleep.

"Boy? Wake up! It's time for you to
leave the hospital."

Still Tom pretended to be asleep. He didn't want to leave the children's ward. Not now. Not ever. It was only when he felt a sharp prod of a finger on his arm that he realised he could no longer pretend.

"But I don't want to go back to my horrible boarding school, sir," pleaded the boy.

"That's fine by me. It's not your headmaster who is here to collect you."

"No?" The boy couldn't think who it could be.

"No. It's your mother and father."

CHAPTER 60

LONG-FORGOTTEN
CHOC ICE

The tall double doors at the end of the children's ward

swung open, and Tom's mum and dad entered.

"TOMMY!" screamed his

mother. She opened her arms and Tom ran towards her.

The woman scooped him up, and gave him the biggest hug. Tom's father was not so good at such moments, and gave his son a manly pat on the back.

"Good to see you, son," he said.

Tom's mum and dad had deep tans from being out in the desert, and were dressed in clothes better suited to being there. It was clear they must have rushed to be here.

"A young girl called Sally phoned us and said we should come and see you," said Mum.

"Sally?!" exclaimed Tom.

"Yes! Lovely girl. Found our phone number in the matron's papers somewhere. Said we should come straight away. Me and your dad were both so worried about you."

"That's Sally – there!" said Tom, pointing to the girl in the far corner of the ward.

"Good morning, Mr and Mrs Charper," called out Sally.

"Good morning, dear!" replied Mum. "You must come and stay with us."

"I'd love that," said Tom.

"Me too," said Sally.

"This **blasted matron woman** put the phone down on us every time we called the ward to try and speak to you!" said Dad. "We were desperate for news of you. The school secretary called us after you were hit on the head playing cricket. We must have called the hospital a hundred times. Now, how is that bump on your head?"

"Much better thanks, Dad," replied Tom with a smile.

"Good, good."

"And, Mum, Dad, I had no idea you wrote to me."

"Every week without fail we sent a letter to St Willet's," said Mum. "Did you not receive them?"

"No. Not one."

"That doesn't make sense," said Dad.

"Mr Thews, my headmaster, **burned them all.**"

Dad looked angrier than Tom had ever seen him before. "If I ever see that man again..."

"STAY CALM, MALCOLM!"

shouted Mum.

Dad breathed heavily for a few moments, and his anger cooled.

"Well, son, rest assured that we are never sending you back to that awful school again," he said.

"YES!" exclaimed Tom.

"We'll all be together from now on," said Mum. "A proper family."

"Come on, son," said Dad.

At that moment Tootsie came in with her breakfast trolley.

"Good morning! Good morning! Good morning to you all!"

"Perfect," muttered Tom to himself. "I'll just miss breakfast."

The boy pulled the curtain back.

"Thomas! Are you leaving us?" she cried.

"Yes. And I am sad to say I won't be staying for breakfast."

"What a terrible shame! And I have everything on my trolley this morning!"

"Of course you do. Another time perhaps."

"Yes. Oh, and I think I found your headmaster, Mr Thews," added Tootsie.

"When? Where?" asked Tom.

"This very morning. In the deep freeze."

"What?"

"Somehow he must have got shut in there overnight."

"He was looking for me in the deep freeze last night! Horrible man! He got his just desserts!" exclaimed

Tom. "So where is he now?"

"Right here!" said Tootsie, whipping a large cloth off her breakfast trolley.

It was indeed Mr Thews lying there, shivering. The man was covered in frost like a long-forgotten choc ice.

"H-h-e-e-l-l-p-p!" mumbled the headmaster. It was all but impossible for him to speak as his teeth were chattering so much.

"I should really take him down to see if the doctors and nurses can thaw him out," said Tootsie.

"There's no rush," replied Tom with a smile.

CHAPTER 61
A TENDER KISS

From out of the matron's office, Thomas Senior limped into the ward. The man had been sleeping after the adventures of last night and looked a little unsteady on his feet. However, on seeing the hospital principal, Sir Quentin Strillers, in the children's ward, he woke up in an instant.

"Oh, erm, um, good morning, Sir Quentin, sir!"

"Ah! Good morning, Thomas Senior."

"So are you absolutely sure I can keep my job, Sir Quentin, sir?"

"No!" replied Sir Quentin. "I am sorry to say I have changed my mind."

"But you said—!" protested Tom.

"I haven't finished yet, boy," snapped Strillers.

"Seeing how happy you make the children, I have decided to change your role at this hospital."

"Oh yes, Sir Quentin, sir?"

"Yes. You are now in charge of the children's ward. I think your title should be 'Doctor of Fun'!"

"Hooray!" the children cheered.

"Oh, thank you, Sir Quentin, sir! I love it!" said Thomas Senior.

As his parents looked on, Tom rushed over to congratulate his friend. The boy threw his arms round the new Doctor of Fun's waist.

"I am so happy for you!" he exclaimed.

"Oh, thank you!" replied the man as the other children rushed over to hug him too. Amber struggled with her broken arms, but found a way.

"But I don't think you should sleep in the basement of the hospital any more," added Sir Quentin.

"No, Sir Quentin, sir," replied Thomas Senior. "I am sorry, sir."

Tootsie approached the man. "Well, if you need somewhere to stay, you can always sleep on my sofa."

"Really?" asked Thomas Senior.

"Yes!"

"That's so very kind of you. I have never had a proper home before."

"Free breakfast included!" replied Tootsie.

"I don't normally eat breakfast," lied the man. "But thank you for the offer of the sofa. That would be truly wonderful."

"Well, it seems a great deal has changed since you were admitted here, boy," began Sir Quentin. "All for the better. I have to say, it was a great pleasure to have you at **LORD FUNT HOSPITAL**, Tim."

"It's Tom," replied Tom.

"Are you sure?"

"Quite sure, sir. And thank you."

"We'd really better get going now, son!" called out Tom's dad.

"Just a moment, Dad!" replied the boy. "I need to say goodbye to my friends."

Tom rushed over to Sally first.

"So your dream did come true after all, Tom," said Sally. "What did I tell you?"

Tom smiled. "All thanks to you, Sally." The boy looked over to his other friends. "I am really going to miss you guys."

"And we are all goin' to miss you," said George. "Though, on the upside, there will be more chocolates for me as I won't 'ave to share them with you any more."

"The Midnight Gang just won't be the same

without you," added Amber.

"I wish you didn't have to go, Tom," said Sally.

Tom placed a tender kiss on the top of his friend's bald head. "I am sorry. But I have to."

"Will you come and visit me here at the hospital?" asked Sally.

"Yes," replied Tom.

"Promise?"

"I promise. And I won't break it this time."

The pair shared a smile.

"And I will never forget you," said Robin. "Sorry, what was your name again?" he joked.

"HA! HA! HA!"

They all laughed.

"Goodbye, gang!" said Tom. "I'll think of you every night at midnight. Wherever we are. Whatever we're doing. Let's meet in our dreams. And have the wildest adventures."

The boy walked towards the double doors. There he took his parents' hands in his and clasped them tight. Now they were a family again, he never wanted to let go.

Tom turned back to take a final look at his friends, before he disappeared from view.

Moments later, the tall doors of the children's ward swung open again. A man in pyjamas marched in, his fingers bandaged up.

"I have a very serious complaint!" Raj announced angrily.

"Wot?" asked George.

"I never did get my takeaway!"

"B-b-but—?"

"Let me repeat my order. Poppadoms..."